MW00943042

GONE
ASTRAY

Linda Marchman

Linda C Marchman

ISBN: 978-1492302575
Linda C. Marchman has had a relationship with cats all her life. Beginning in elementary school she began rescuing stray and homeless cats, trying to find appropriate homes for them. She is a self-proclaimed "cat lady" and some may think of her as a "crazy cat lady" but that doesn't faze her. Her love of felines has brought a number of them to spend their lives with her and her husband, Rex. Thanks to her patient demeanor, many ferals have become beloved pets and contented house cats. She believes that all cats can be tamed somewhat so they can coexist with humans.

Gone Astray is her first novel, one that she has been thinking of writing for many years. She currently lives in Charlottesville, Virginia with Rex and a houseful of cats.

ISBN: 1492302570

"Gone Astray" is a fictional account of a kitten's adventures as she is shuttled around in her younger years and her decision to run away and live the wild life as she grows up. As a pretty calico, she begins life precariously and meets a cast of "cataracters" along the way. Although fiction, many of the events could have actually happened. The reader will gain much insight into a cat's life through the interaction of "Kitty" with other cats, dogs, wild animals, and humans.

ACKNOWLEDGEMENTS

Several people were instrumental in helping me write and complete Gone Astray. With their encouragement and guidance, the book has finally taken shape and hopefully will be read and remembered by many as a story of a brave and adventurous little cat.

In order of their involvement:

Rex Marchman, my husband of many years who read through the book in record time and pronounced it "very good."

Jane Barr, my grammarian, who suggested changes that made the writing easier to comprehend and provided guidance in making the action flow in an orderly manner.

Jewell Bailey, my friend and fellow cat lover, who offered tips and inspiration through the entire process.

Caitlin Marie Collins, my sweet and favorite granddaughter, who was instrumental in formatting the text for <u>Gone Astray</u> to produce it as a paperback.

TABLE OF CONTENTS

IN THE WOODS AND HUNGRY

I woke up cold, tired and hurting. My paws felt like they had been subjected to shards of broken glass and in fact my left front pad was crusted over with dried blood. The temperature must have been in the lower 20s the night before and even though my coat had thickened over the past few months, it still did not provide the insulation I needed to keep warm during the nights. But the biggest factor in my discomfort was the gnawing hunger that never seemed to go away. I was always hungry. Even if I was able to catch a meal, it wasn't satisfying for very long. The occasional mouse or winter bird provided just a portion of what my thinning body needed to sustain itself.

First thing to attend to was my injured paw. The soothing motion of licking it helped to ease the hurt somewhat, but it still was painful to walk on. The memories of the past few days came flooding back and it was with alarm that I remembered them. I looked around and saw brown. Brown leaves, brown dirt, brown tree bark. The hollow in the old fallen oak tree provided a poor shelter from the elements and the leaves crisped and crackled as I reached out a tentative paw. How did I happen to find myself in this predicament? The air had a frozen touch and I knew before long it would be winter with all the accompanying hardships.

I had been tracked by a coyote for several days, eluding him the best I could, scrambling up trees, sleeping in the precarious branches while he patrolled the ground underneath. He kept watch while I lost sleep, ever wakeful to his predatory actions. His mean black eyes burned with a killing desire as he gazed at me balancing on the branch. I thought I could outlast him because at some point his attention would be distracted by some small rodent that was more accessible than I was. For two days and nights he did not leave the area even though it rained a merciless downpour one night. He seemed impervious to the elements, while I was suffering and my coat was soaked through. I tried to outstare him, narrowing my eyes and trying to make myself look larger than my measly eight pounds. He was a thin, poor specimen of an animal, with a devious look and a long, dog-like snout with appropriately-named canines gleaming wickedly. His fur was patchy and reddish-gray, not well-groomed. He watched me constantly, as I watched him. I felt fortunate that those of his species were unable to climb trees as my instinct for survival kept me awake and alert.

Finally yesterday, he seemed to perk up at some minute rustling in the leaves. Oh, maybe I was going to survive this latest episode after all. Ears bent forward, he sniffed the ground intently, as his body tensed for the pounce. The unfortunate gray mouse poked its head up from bit of tree branch to smell the pungent air. Little white whiskers and a twitching nose tentatively showed above the leaf layer. That was all the coyote needed as he sprang up and then down to grab the mouse, shake it vigorously, until it became limp in the coyote's grasp. Sparing the details, the coyote was able to enjoy his breakfast under my watchful gaze. He even consumed the bones, noisily crunching the marrow. I had no choice but to keep my eyes on him.

I figured he would be napping soon and my prediction came true. Seeming to lose interest in me, he slunk away to find a soft place on which to lay his skinny bones. I hate coyotes almost as much as predatory dogs and this one proved to be almost too much of a close call. I could still smell his dog-like odor but gradually it became faint as he left the area. My body relaxed somewhat and I was able to groom my coat. My paw hurt from running from the coyote, but I felt it was now safe to attempt to back down the tree and find a safer place to hunt.

On the ground, I needed to drink, but where was a good source of clean water? Lifting my head, I tried to smell the air for a whiff of water. My acute hearing led me to a small spring, which bubbled up out of the ground. The dirt was annoyingly damp under my feet, but I bent my head to a pool and lapped up a good amount of the sweet liquid. No chemicals in this water and for that, I was grateful. Small things had become big blessings in the past years since I had been on my own.

My sore paw aching, and stretching to relieve the muscle stiffness, I wandered in the boggy bottom, getting my feet wet and dirty. Always on the alert, I honed my sense of smell on the decaying leaves, the sharp air, and a myriad of other unidentified odors so peculiar to a formerly indoor cat. My exposure to and lack of recognition of such smells still astounded me even after so long living in the wild. My experience prior to my outdoor adventures had been as a young cat, mostly confined to the aromas of canned food, sumptuous dinners on the stove, the smell of a warm person and fresh laundry straight from the dryer. Oh, and some occasional fresh catnip from a garden, which intoxicated me and sent me into spasms of unbridled joy. One memory came back just then and it was of catnip being dried in the microwave oven just for my benefit. How wonderful that day was! The whole house was permeated with the pleasing scent of concentrated catnip! I had wanted to jump right in the microwave, but was dissuaded by my person who discouraged me from walking on the countertops. I walked on them at night when she was asleep anyway, sometimes licking the remains of whatever was cooked for dinner and hadn't been cleaned off the counter. Other memories of food brought me back to my present situation, which was not satisfactory, to say the least. I hadn't eaten in at least three days and my body was crying out for something substantial. It hadn't taken long to acquire a taste for wild food after I went outside. Birds, lizards, grasshoppers, rodents and even the occasional rabbit held a special appeal for me, in spite of being raised on dry and canned cat food. The problem was that there were never enough of them to satisfy my constant craving. Most of my time was spent searching for food and catching it. But I was still quick and agile and my claws were sharp and lethal so I wasn't starving, at least not yet.

I was a bit reluctant to leave the shelter of the fallen oak, not that it provided that much protection, but I was unsure whether I would be able to find anywhere else suitable to hide myself. My coat is a mixture of colors: black, white, and orange, which makes a pretty good camouflage. I am a calico with a turtle-like back of patches of color while my underside is primarily white. I was doing my best to keep myself clean, but my white underbelly was showing an orange tint here and there from the clay and a few Velcro-like seeds were stuck in it. The fur on my face is a jumble of tri-color but could not be described as typical. Most calicos are unique in their fur markings. My eyes are a pale green, the color of fresh celery, not that I cared for celery. The palette of fur shades helped to conceal me somewhat in the woods, but in the open, I am very visible, like a walking, crumpled up magazine cover.

Since it was morning and prime time for hunting, I began to stalk through the base of the tree trunks, the low-hanging shrub branches and forest debris. Carefully I placed my feet where I would not be heard, avoiding small twigs and freshly-fallen leaves. My paw hurt and I limped slightly. I must have stepped on something sharp that cut my tender pad. I needed all my senses to be in top shape to survive and a sore paw was indeed a setback.

At the edge of the woods was a field with some dried wildflowers bent to the ground. Since the freeze several weeks ago, most of the vegetation had died and the earth was readying itself to hibernate for the cold winter months. The grasses that I liked to munch on were now brown and crispy and not fit for consumption. There were still weeds, of course, but they held little appeal for me. Grass always helped my digestive tract and now it would be many months before the tender blades would begin to show forth in the spring. The field was one that was used for grazing and I smelled the unmistakable odor of cows. Really overwhelming it was. Luckily, the wind was blowing away from me so I wasn't overcome with the fragrance of cow manure. I was not afraid of cows, even though they were huge compared to my petite size. They were not threatening since they were herbivores, and not interested in cats. Taking stock of the situation, I continued to cleanse my paw, hoping it would heal soon. In the distance, I saw several black and white cows placidly grazing on some newly spread hay. How nice that a person would provide them with food throughout the winter. It brought back memories when my person would do the same for me. A warm lap and a soft bed to sleep on were now far away remembrances. Well, that was in the past.

Across the field was a large pond through which the spring fed. The water was fresh and there were many tall water grasses lining the edges. Knowing what I did about water sources, I guessed that other animals would be drawn to it for refreshment. The main drawback was that the cows also drank from it, bathed in it and probably used it as a litter box. My tongue would never touch water like that!

Suddenly, out of the corner of my eye, I saw movement among the water reeds on the shoreline. Geese! They were making no effort to conceal themselves; they were just waddling around, heading for the water. Larger than a rabbit, they seemed sort of clumsy, but I knew they could take flight instantly. I thought about what a breakfast of goose would taste like and decided

I would like to try it. Mmm, foie gras! I crouched down and started stealthily creeping closer to the geese. There were five of them in a row. As I got closer, they seemed to sense that something was wrong. Maybe the wind had shifted. They began waddling faster, trying to make it into the water where they probably knew I wouldn't follow. I twitched my tail and was getting excited, as my hunting instinct kicked in. In earnest I started pursuing them. Just as I was almost within paw reach, they lifted off in a graceful way, flying toward the opposite edge and then up and up in a line, like a group of fighter jets. How discouraging! My efforts were wasted. My hunger was unabated. My goose breakfast dreams vanished. My paw still hurt. The cows placidly looked over at me, mystified as to my predicament. Their large brown eyes gazed at me, sizing me up and decided that I was not a threat. One calf bawled for his mama, found her and started suckling immediately. So convenient, a ready-made snack provider. How peaceful they seemed, unlike myself, constantly on the prowl, alert to any dangers. Oh, to be a cow! But then I thought of the end result and the unsuspecting cows. Steaks, hamburgers, leather. Maybe not.

Still hungry, I limped back to the woods, hoping for something, anything, to appease my pangs. Sharpening my claws on a tree trunk, I began to feel a bit better. Flexing my claws and using the trunk to mark the place where I had been, I left my scent. Scents are very important in the wild. It's like reading a newspaper. You can tell who had been there, what type of animal it was, and how long ago it had passed by. Some cats scent-mark in other ways, but I usually just used my claws or the glands on my cheek pads to announce my comings and goings. In these woods, I had caught the scent of several other cats a few months ago, but not lately. I wondered where those cats were now. I hoped that nothing bad had happened. So many times cats are the targets of mean-spirited people. Many cats are too trusting and will go wherever someone puts down food, even if the food has been poisoned. Why would someone want to poison a cat? We are not destructive. We don't kill many birds; our hunting instinct is a natural feeling and we must follow it. The habits of humans are what is causing a decline in the bird population, not cats. We are beautiful and add charm and grace to people's lives.

Back in the breakfast mode, I picked up a mouse scent. Following my nose, the scent grew stronger, close to where the coyote had devoured the other one. There must be a nest of them nearby! My feelings about eating other animals are thus: Cats are higher up on the food chain than some lower-ranked animals and we must have protein in our diet. I was hungry and the mice were close. It wasn't hard to catch one, throw it up in the air, play with it for a while, and finally settle down to eat my breakfast. I felt sorry for its family, but mice reproduce at an amazing rate and I figured there would soon be many more to take its place.

Washing my face, then my paws, then my coat, I was ready for a nap. But where? I didn't want to go back to the oak tree, but just at that moment, I saw a streak of pale orange flash by under the oak trunk. Was that a cat? It wasn't a pumpkin orange, but more of a pale tan color. I froze mid-lick with my sore paw held up in the air. Very soon I saw another streak. Two cats? These were small flashes, not full-size like me. Could it be kittens? Right here in the woods? I was new to the area so I guessed it was possible that the other cats I had scented were living in the forest. The sun was coming out and briefly dappled some light in the woodland. Hopefully it would warm up so I could absorb some healing rays, so important to cats.

Just then two little kittens appeared in plain sight, playing with each other's tails, chasing, romping, scampering, jumping and tumbling. Wow! I had mainly tried to stay away from other cats in my time outside. My independence had made me stronger and more self-reliant. One never knew about other cats and their temperament. But these little ones were fascinating. They did not realize I was watching them. Arching backs, they stalked each other as if they were tiny, pale tigers. They were almost pink in color, pale khaki or light brown with tabby stripes all over their bodies. Miniature cat twins, kittenish playfulness. Petite chatons. A white butterfly flitted by, capturing their attention. Kittens paid attention to the smallest things - a bug, the movement of a flower, the wind ruffling their fur. These kittens probably weren't even six weeks old, but were curious as the proverbial cat.

A memory returned from my kittenhood. Born in a closet with my siblings, I was warm and cared for by my mama. Soft cushions and blankets shielded us from the hard floor. As I grew stronger, I played with my brothers and sisters just like these two were doing. So long ago! We were all so cute back then. One day after my mama had quit nursing us, we were taken away. I never saw my mama or my brothers and sisters again. Did I miss them? Yes, I did, but there were so many new experiences in store for me that the memory had become dim. Fuzzy kittens playing in the sun made me feel happy. I didn't feel happy very much anymore since I went outside. Outside there were many challenges, the most urgent one being the issue of hunger.

But, on the other paw, I was free. Free to do whatever I wanted. Free to go wherever I wished and free from people making choices that impacted my life. The feeling was exhilarating. The feeling of partial contentment was enough for now. My roaming never took me too far, however. I usually stayed within a short radius of my home base. My former home was far away and I didn't want to make the attempt to travel the distance for several reasons. But there were adventures in store for me soon.

The wind shifted and I knew my scent would soon be discovered. I also knew that there might be a protective mama watching her babies. I crouched, trying to blend in with the fall leaves.

FIRST HOME

My first home after I was taken from my mother was with a family who didn't need a cat. The family consisted of a father, mother, and two elementary school-aged boys. The parents were away most every day working and the boys were at school or at some type of ball game practice. I was left alone in the house to amuse myself. Being a kitten, I was naturally curious and wanted to explore every nook. But I was shut up in a laundry room with only a washer and dryer to keep me company. I guess the people didn't want me to scratch the furniture or make messes in the house. I was given water and dry and canned food. I couldn't run off all my kitten energy and was bored. I was frustrated with the confines of the laundry room. My toys consisted of a tennis ball and a marble, which I had batted under the washing machine where I couldn't get at them. What a life. Why did these people adopt a kitten if they didn't want to pay any attention to me? Every once in a while I was let out of the room and the boys played roughly with me, like I was a dog. A dog! I was handled harshly, not gently in the way I deserved. Once, they even played catch with me, throwing me back and forth like I was a baseball. I was terrified and my claws snagged one of the boys' fingers. He screeched and dropped me. I ran through the house and hid under a couch. They chased me and I crouched in a corner trying to make myself invisible. They couldn't reach me so one found a broom and started to sweep me out. Not being familiar with brooms, I was scared. I put out my paw to stop it, but the bristles poked at me relentlessly. The broom swiped again and again, hurting me. Finally I was rescued by the parents who put a stop to the broom poking. The couch was moved and I was picked up and put back into the laundry room. Thus ended my first adventure in the house.

Several days later, I was anxious and had so much pent-up energy that I just wanted to get out and run free and play. Kittens need a lot of playtime and room to stretch their legs and flex their developing muscles. I had too little room in which to do this and no toys to play with. Finally someone threw in a small catnip mouse. The catnip was old and, since I was so young, not intoxicating. I batted it and pushed it around on

the floor until it went under the washing machine. I
tried and tried to reach it with my small paw, to no
avail. So there I was, back in the same position with
no diversions. But there was a window, where I spent
most of my days watching the events happening outside. I saw an occasional bird, which I would have loved
to chase. Butterflies flew by and I'd reach up, but my
paw only touched the window. Once or twice a day
someone would come by walking a dog. This was my
first encounter with a dog, even though it was outside
and I was inside. The dog seemed to be well-behaved
and walked on a leash. They didn't notice me and I was
glad. I inherently knew I should be afraid of dogs, but
I wasn't sure why.

A couple of times a week the woman would come
in to do laundry. The sound of both the washer and
dryer was loud and hurt my ears. The woman would
say a few words to me, but other than that, did not pay
much attention to me. Why was I here? Why did these
people adopt me? I knew there must be something better, but I was powerless to do anything about it. I tried
to touch her shoestrings, but she moved my paws aside.
Once I put my claws in her pants and she said, "No!" in
a loud voice that scared me. I hid behind the washer
after that.

The dry cat food and canned food the woman
plopped in my dish twice a day was adequate, but she
never spoke to me when she set my dish down. There

was a litter box in the corner and I knew how to use it. I wished it was scooped out more frequently, but I couldn't complain. I was just plain lonely. I started sleeping more during the daytime. I did love to lie in the sunlight that shone through the window in the afternoons. Cats need sunlight, just like people do. Sometimes I could see a butterfly flit by and it aroused my interest. My days were boring and I was bored. What a life for a little kitten.

I was glad that the boys mostly left me alone and did not try to play baseball with me again. I could hear them stomping around the house and slamming doors when they came home. They were at school during the day and the parents were at work. In the evenings everyone was home, unless the boys had a game and then the house was quiet again because the parents attended the games.

One day, the woman did not shut the laundry room door securely. I waited until the house was empty and I pushed the door open so I could extend my head through the crack. I wiggled until I was finally outside the laundry room. Ahh! I had the whole house to myself to explore! I saw the couch where I hid before and I remembered the broom and how painful it was. I stretched out my claws on the side of the couch and it was a wonderful feeling. I scratched the couch and snagged my claw in the fabric, but I knew no one would notice. I could pull myself up on the couch and play hide and seek in the pillows. I could even chase my own tail on the couch seat. One of the pillows fell on the floor, but I didn't care. I was still small enough that I could only jump up about a foot so I had to climb up on the upholstered chairs. I could smell the scents of the people. I rubbed the sides of my face on the chairs so they would know I had been there.

I made my way into the kitchen where there were many delicious aromas lingering. I could smell hamburger and milk. The milk was probably left over from someone's breakfast. There must have been a pile of dishes in the sink, but there was no way for me to reach them. I sat there for a few moments inhaling the smells of people food.

A staircase led up to more rooms upstairs, but I was too small to navigate it. I would have loved to run up and down, but I had to content myself with just looking at it. But for a short time, I was free of the laundry room. I ran back and forth from room to room. I peered out some different windows onto a lawn and some trees. After a while, I fell asleep in the sunlight on the dining room carpet. I don't know how long I was there, but I was awakened by a slamming door. Trouble, I thought. I hid under a big wooden piece of furniture. Heavy footsteps pounded up the stairs. A backpack was thrown down. Some music started playing. I guess it was called "music" but to my tender ears, it was just loud annoying noise. I thought my best bet was to stay hidden in case baseball boy took an inclination to practicing with me. A while later, the door slammed again and there were more heavy footsteps running up the stairs. Some loud voices from the boys reached my ears and I shrunk back into the corner under the furniture. I knew it would be dinnertime soon because I was getting hungry, but I didn't know what would happen. The boys didn't know I was awol and for that I was glad. Presently the woman came home and started preparing dinner. I saw her pass by my hiding place and she must have seen that the laundry room door was ajar. She started calling my name, "Kitty." Kitty! What an unimaginative name.

"Kitty!" "Kitty!" I drew myself up into a ball. She told the boys to come downstairs to start looking for me. Reluctantly, they both trudged down and began to look under the furniture. Uh oh. I knew they'd find me sooner or later. Please, not the broom again! Eventually, one boy saw my tail moving and I saw his grubby little hand reaching for me. I pulled myself tighter. He couldn't quite grab me and I was so hoping it would not be the broom again. It was something equally bad - a metal yardstick sweeping under the sideboard, hitting my paws and hurting them. I moved slightly towards him and as he reached for me again, I quickly swiped his finger with my claw.

"Ooooww!" I must have drawn blood because he continued yelling and then the woman came running.

I figured my time on earth was probably coming to an end so I crawled out and looked frantically for another place where I could hide. But the woman was faster and roughly grabbed me and then angrily shoved me back into the laundry room. My little body hurt where she had pinched me but as least I was safe again.

That night I heard murmurs about me coming from the man and woman. Phrases like, "Scratched his hand again,"

"Don't really need a cat,"

"Maybe a dog would help." A dog? A dog would help? Help me? Were these people crazy?

A few more days passed with no further incidents. The door remained firmly shut. I started putting my paw under the door just because it felt good and it made the door rattle somewhat. I don't know why I did this, but it seemed like the cat thing to do. Once or twice when the people were home, and they heard the rattling door, they'd come by and knock sharply on it and I would withdraw my paw. At least they didn't step on it. Again, I heard talk at night about me.

"Annoying."

"Needs a playmate." Yes, I would like a playmate. Another kitten would be perfect, but I had the feeling that wouldn't be part of the plan. Even a person who liked cats and would say a few kind words to me and pay me a bit of attention would be good. But that was not to be.

Several days later, I could feel excitement in the house. Something was going on but I didn't know what it could be. The people left in the morning and were gone for a few hours. Suddenly the door slammed open and I heard a scrabbling noise which frightened me. The boys were shouting and laughing and I was scared so I hid behind the washer. The scrabbling came closer and then I smelled it. I smelled a dog. It was a puppy smell, sort of fresh, but definitely doggy. The laundry room door started banging and it was flung open. With a rush of wind, a puppy squirted his way into the room all sniffs and noses. I crouched and tried to make myself smaller, but the puppy found me anyway. This puppy was large, much larger than a kitten and larger than a grown cat. I'm not sure what type of dog this was, but it definitely was an active one. I arched my back when he saw me. He backed away a few inches and then lunged at me. I hissed. Hissed! I didn't know I could hiss, but it just escaped my lips. This scared him a bit, but not for long. He lunged again and I tried to make myself look as big as possible, which, for a three month old kitten was not very large. My fur was standing out and I could feel my skin crawl. My pupils were dilated and I dared not blink. The boys looked at me and howled. They thought this was funny. A terrified little kitten is not to be laughed at. And I was terrified. I turned to the side so the dog would see my profile, which I thought made me look bigger. This big black bundle of energy was all I had hoped I would not ever have to encounter. Lunge, lunge! Hiss, spit! I tried to warn him not to come any closer, but being a dog, he didn't take the hint. I growled a little kitten growl, which was another new experience for me. It didn't faze him. Lunge, and his paw hit me. I withdrew as far as I could. He pushed his way behind the washer to get at me and finally I had enough. I extended my claw and slashed his nose. Yelp! Oww! Howwwlll! What was I to do? Just let him mangle me?

One of the boys grabbed him and dragged him out from behind the washer, exclaiming how mean I was and oh, poor little puppy. His nose was bleeding a bit so they took him away and shut the door. I was shaking and my kitten heart was beating furiously. My skin tingled and my fur felt almost alive. My fur eventually settled back down, but I really was petrified. Was this dog going to live here? In this house where I lived? Oh, surely not!

I was lazily looking out the window of the laundry room, watching for the occasional bird. This was my main entertainment. Suddenly I saw the puppy come bounding out of a side door, romping in the grass. Bounding to and fro, chasing imaginary sticks, the dog was having a big time just being a dog. Out came the boys, running and roughhousing with the puppy. They all looked like they were enjoying the sunshine and the freedom of the great outdoors immensely. One boy produced a rubber bone and the dog grabbed one end and shook it playfully. The boy threw it across the yard and the dog ran after it, picked it up and ran in the opposite direction. The boys chased the dog and the game continued for some time. Finally the dog began to wind down and lay down, panting from the exercise. The boys patted him and scratched his head. The dog rolled over on his back, exposing his underside. Oh, what a joy it must be to run and jump and play and to feel the cool grass under one's paws. The sun's rays cast short shadows, indicating it was midday. I could almost feel the sun warming my fur, lulling me to sleep as I pretended to be outside.

The boys spotted me before the puppy did. They seemed to be having a secret conversation and then laughed and pointed at me. All three of them started running toward me, toward the window and I jumped down and hid behind the washer. How much fun is it to torment a poor little kitten?

I knew trouble was coming when I heard the door slam and heavy footsteps coming my way.

"Here, Kitty, Kitty," called one of them. I tried to flatten myself and become invisible.

"Kitty, Kitty, Kitty! Come on out to play!" I didn't want to play. Play for me had a bad memory and I would just as soon hide from everyone. A hand reached around the washer and pulled me out. I was taken through the house and through a door into the sunlight. The sun felt so good. I was deposited on the grass. What a feeling! I stretched my paws out and felt the grass tickling my pads.

I could have spent a lot of time just being there, but then I saw the black ball of fur start to race toward me. Evidently he did not remember the nose-scratching I gave him. He stopped short of me and began to circle, lunging in the same way as before. He started to act crazy, running away a few feet and then back in my direction. What was it with this dog? He obviously thought I was another toy to be tossed around like the rubber bone. The boys were having a good time just watching the interaction between kitten and puppy. I, on the other hand was purely miserable. I arched my back, trying to make myself look bigger. I looked like a razorback. My fur stood on end and my tail was a bottle-brush, but the puppy continued his game. How much longer would this continue? Finally the puppy touched my tail with his paw. I swung around and hissed to no avail. I had to get out of there.

Guardedly, I looked around and saw a tree at the side of the yard. I started backing up toward it, but my progress was slow, as the puppy impeded my movements. I decided to make a break for it and with a burst of speed, I raced toward the tree. Boys and dog followed me. Using my sharp little claws, I scrambled up the trunk. I could climb! I was out of danger! Upward I went, resting on a low limb. The puppy bounced off the trunk and the boys began to reach for me. I could see that I needed to climb higher, so I grabbed the trunk and hoisted myself up to a much higher branch. I could look down on all three and they could not get to me. The puppy was racing around the base of the tree, trying to climb it. Ha ha! Not very smart. The tree was not very big, but it was large enough to hold me. One boy tried to shimmy up the trunk, but only made it to the first lower limb. The tree began to bend under his weight. He prudently thought better of this idea and sprang back to the ground.

"Kitty, come down!"

"Come on, Kitty, let's play!" I watched every move from my high perch. No way was I coming down. I settled in the crook of the branch and gazed upon my enemies.

"Kitty! Kitty!" I ignored them as much as possible. The tree was a good idea. I was out of their reach and out of the dog's mad frenzy. I looked up to see a bird on the top limb, furtively looking around. A bird! Almost within my reach! I slowly began to climb higher but the bird saw and heard my movement and flew away. I was almost up to the top of the tree and the sun was filtering down through the leaves. A slight breeze ruffled my fur and it felt wonderful.

"Kitty!" I saw the boys begin to search the ground. What was going on now? One picked up a small rock and tossed it in my direction. They were trying to hit me with rocks! More rocks were thrown my way, missing me, but a few coming too close. Would I ever get a break?

After several minutes of rock throwing, I saw a lady jogging down the street, heading in our direction. She was wearing running shoes, a t-shirt, and shorts. Her blonde hair was tied back in a ponytail. As she came closer, she began to take in what was happening. Stopping short of the yard, she saw my fur colors high up in the tree and watched the boys throwing rocks in my direction. I could see she was angry. She stomped over to the boys and started yelling at them to stop.

"What are you doing?" she demanded.

"Our cat is up the tree and won't come down," one boy replied.

"So, you think the best way to get her down is to throw rocks at her?" Both boys put down their stockpile of rocks and looked sheepish.

"Don't ever throw rocks at your cat again! Does your mother know what you're doing?" the lady inquired.

"No, she's not home yet."

She said, "You boys need to take your puppy and go play inside. You could have seriously hurt the kitten. She will come down when she is ready."

The lady waited with her hands on her hips while the boys gathered the puppy up and walked slowly back into the house. She looked up through the branches at me and I looked down at her. She may have thought that I would be trying to climb back down the tree now that the coast was clear, but I was safe on my perch and was not going anywhere. I knew this lady had just helped me and may have saved me from a bad situation, but frankly, I was not sure how to get back down the tree, having never climbed one before. Should I go forward or backward? Would my little claws hold me? I had a lot of patience and knew my outdoor time would be limited once the parents came home. Might as well enjoy myself on my branch. I put my head down on my front paws and kept one eye on the lady. She continued to watch me for several minutes and then continued on her jog, occasionally looking back to see if I would attempt the climb down.

A few hours passed and the sun moved across the sky to the west. It was a bit warm in the tree and I wished I had some water to drink. I was also getting hungry. The boys and the puppy were nowhere to be seen. Cautiously I put out my front paw and then a back leg to try to grip the tree trunk. My foot slipped and I decided to stay put. A few pieces of bark fell to the ground. This might be harder than I thought. Better stay where I was.

As the sun continued its journey toward the horizon, I saw a car come down the street and turn into the driveway. Must be a parent coming home from work. The car door opened and the woman leaned across the seat and took out a briefcase and a purse before slamming the door shut. She went into the house. I had a feeling of unease but couldn't quite put my paw on it.

Presently, the woman came out of the house with the boys who started pointing in my direction. She looked up and spied me in the upper branch.

"Kitty! Kitty!"

"Come here, Kitty!" I just stared at her.

"Why is the cat up in the tree?" she asked.

"Well, we were playing with her and Beau and she just ran up the tree."

I could see the wheels turning in her head as she processed this information.

"You mean you put her out here in the yard with the dog?"

"We just thought Beau wanted to play with her."

"Well, how do you think we're going to get her down out of the tree?" she asked tightly.

"Maybe she'll just jump down."

"Jump down from the top of the tree?" The woman's mouth pulled into a narrow line.

"Maybe we could get the ladder and climb up to get her," one boy suggested.

"I am not climbing up the ladder!"

This was one angry woman. "We'll have to wait until your father gets home." With that, she stomped back into the house.

The boys looked up at me again and I narrowed my eyes.

"Uh oh, I think we're in trouble."

"Kitty, Kitty, come down! I'll give you some cat food." Ha! That was an old trick and I wasn't falling for it. I knew as my punishment I'd be put back in the laundry room by myself for a long time. The tree branch was much better than the laundry room. Here I was, in the fresh air, outside, with a good view of the street and other yards. I was relatively safe as long as they didn't use the ladder. I looked away and the boys retreated to the house.

About an hour later, another car pulled into the driveway and the man climbed out. He didn't look around, but just walked tiredly into the house. Presently I heard some loud voices in the house and the door banged open and the man stepped out of the door. He inclined his head and tried to find me among the leaves. I tried to make myself invisible, but my colors gave me away. He sighed.

"I want you to come down now," he commanded. I surmised by the tone of his voice that he was used to giving orders and being obeyed. Cats don't respond well to commands and especially not to rough talk. I scrunched down flat on the limb.

"Ok, we'll just leave you up there until you come down" and with that, he didn't glance at me again, but just went back inside.

I was tired and hungry and thirsty. I had had an exhausting day. I catnapped for a while and it started to get dark. I could smell odors of food cooking and then I knew the people were eating dinner inside. Even the dog was eating and I was out here starving. They must not have cared whether I came down the tree or not because no one came outside to check on me. Conceivably I could have clawed my way down and run away and they wouldn't have known it. I started to feel lonely and discarded.

The darkness came on slowly and I hadn't moved. After a while I saw a flashlight and the beam pointed up at me. I squinted because the bright light hurt my eyes. The light went out and the door shut.

The night sounds gradually became more numerous. A few tree frogs began to croak. A frog chorus enlivened the dusk. Small rustlings in the leaves on the ground made me perk up. The night smells became more vivid. With each new sound I swiveled my ears to locate it. A swooshing swept by and I knew it must be a bat! The bat was catching its dinner. Small flying insects buzzed quickly. The beating of a moth's wings attracted my attention to a flowering shrub on the ground. The bat flew by again. This was all a new experience for me as I had been inside all my life. I began to feel alive. The noises were very loud because I have such sensitive hearing. These creatures were out feeding themselves and I was stuck up in the tree. My dinner time was well past and the people in the house were quiet so they must have been going to bed. I knew the puppy had been fed and was probably in his bed in the boys' room.

The air cooled and more insects buzzed around the tree. A mosquito landed on my fur and tried to bite me, but I brushed it away. It grew darker and my senses awakened. Dozing time was over and I was fully aware of noises, aromas, and even animal whispers. The people must have either forgotten about me or given up on the hope that I would descend the tree this late. Even if I came down, what would I have done? Where would I go? I guessed I could wait on the porch until morning, but I was unsure of how to climb down the tree bark to the ground. I stayed put on my perch. I could feel my eyes adjust to the darkness and I began to see the night creatures. The one moth became a flurry of moths, flying around the night-blooming flowers. Where did they go in the daylight? I supposed they rested, unlike butterflies that were active in the day.

After some time, and much sensory stimulation, the moon appeared over the roof of the house across the street. I had only ever seen the moon through an indoor window and I was drawn to its quiet beauty. Almost full, it illuminated the yard and cast moon shadows.

A moving shadow appeared from behind a bush in the neighbor's yard. It was a cat! I could see it sniffing the air. Big and black with a white bib, it stopped under my tree and scratched the trunk to leave its scent. It was a "cow" cat, marked like a bovine. My eyes gleamed in the moonlight and the cat peered up to see me watching it. I knew this was a male and he was curious about me. My fur began to expand as I continued to watch him. His eyes narrowed to slits as he crouched at the base of the tree. What did he want with me? I was just a kitten, stuck way up in a tree. I didn't mean him any harm. He settled down and tucked his paws underneath his body but continued to keep me in his line of sight. The moon moved overhead. It must have been after midnight.

After several hours, not too far away, I heard dogs barking. The black cat also heard them and turned toward the sound. Suddenly, he sprang up and ran across the yard and disappeared under the neighbor's car. Then I saw them. Three dogs running in a pack, crossed the road, yipping and yelling, and surrounded the car where the cat had hidden. Dogs in packs really scared me, not that I had that much experience with them, but instinctively I knew they were bad news. Howling with delight, they began to try to squirm under the car. The black cat hissed. He was under the wheel well, on top of a wheel, close enough to the dogs, and barely protected from their jaws. I wondered why these dogs were running loose at night. Didn't they have homes? I felt helpless. The dogs made such a racket I thought they would surely wake up the people in the house. And just as that thought crossed my mind, lights came on in my house. The man came running out, barefoot, and wearing only a t-shirt and shorts. A shock ran up my spine as I saw he was carrying a gun! It was only a pellet gun, but he aimed it at the dog pack and shot two or three pellets in the direction of his neighbor's car. One pellet dinged the side door and the man cursed. Scared by the noise, the dogs finally ran off. I didn't know what had happened to the black and white cat. The man walked into the neighbor's yard and scrunched down to look under the car, but didn't see the cat. He must have thought the dogs were after me! Another swear word and he went back into the house, presumably to resume his sleep.

Oh, so much excitement for a little cat! Actually, it was too much excitement. I really wanted to be back in the laundry room, safe and secure. The outdoors wasn't as enticing as I had thought it would be after all.

Sometime before the dawn broke, I heard the black and white cat jump down from the wheel and run up the street from where he had come. He didn't give me a backward glance as I saw his black tail disappear down the road. I had spent my first night outdoors and as I looked back, there were good and bad things that I stored away in my cat mind for further use. I was very hungry and longed for some kitten food and my little bed inside the house. My wishes were not to come true for when it was light enough for people to be up and about, I saw the man come around the house. He first looked under the neighbor's car and saw that I wasn't there. Then he looked up and noticed me, still on the same branch. He went around to the back yard and returned with a ladder. It was a tall ladder, tall enough to almost reach me.

He laid the ladder down and called, "Kitty! Kitty!" I just watched him. He had a sour expression on his face. He went into the house and shortly returned with a box, a bit bigger than a shoebox. Setting up the ladder close to the tree's trunk, he began to climb up toward me. He was coming to get me! Up and up he came. Closer and closer until he was within an arm's distance. He reached out to grab me and it scared me so of course, I reached out to scratch him. I nicked his finger and I heard the swear word he used the previous night. Finally he pinched me along the scruff of my neck and I dangled precariously in his hand. I squirmed and he held me close to his chest, trying to balance himself with one hand on the ladder and one hand gripping me. Descending the ladder slowly, one rung at a time, at last we reached the ground. Now, maybe I could go back inside and eat my breakfast and rest in my little bed.

But no! The man put me in the box and closed the lid. I was trapped! I could barely turn around and it was dark in there. He brought me into the house and I could hear tape ripping as he taped the top shut so I couldn't escape. What was to happen to me now? My little heart was beating so fast and I was so frightened. I was a prisoner in the box. There were no air holes and I hoped I wouldn't be in there for long. The box was picked up and taken outside and then put into the car. The man got in and started the engine. I panicked since I was not very familiar with cars, except for the short ride from my birthplace to this home. I was confined in a small box in a large, moving machine. I started crying and scratching the sides of the box. As the car traveled down the road, my cries got louder and more poignant. Why me? Where was I going? It was dark and scary in there! The car's movement upset my stomach and I balled up in a corner. I cried and cried. The man said nothing to ease my anxiety. He drove and I howled. I was so distraught that I thought I was going to be physically sick. Then the car turned into a gravel driveway and stopped. I heard him say, "This is where we part ways, Kitty."

THE WOODS

Shortly, the two kittens scampered away through the woods. I relaxed and licked my paw again and again. I knew I would have to rest it so it would have a chance to heal, but I felt like I needed to be on the move. I stretched out my body and that felt good. Maybe I could take a short catnap. I went back to the tree trunk and wriggled into the decaying wood hole. I was partially hidden and felt fairly safe. The wind shifted and I could detect fall and the coming winter. I was not looking forward to another cold frozen winter outdoors. I couldn't migrate south like birds or Monarch butterflies; I was basically stuck in this area and had to endure at least three or four cold months. The previous winter was very bad. The temperatures were below normal for most of the time and I was constantly cold. Cats hate to be cold and I was so very cold.

The snow and sleet and ice wore me down and food was scarce. My fur was always wet and I looked terrible. I never could seem to warm up and to ease my misery, I remembered my good times indoors where there was heat and food and comfort. I began to doze and dream of those better times. My dreams took me back to my other home where I was wanted and loved and cherished. Would I ever experience such good fortune again or was I destined to be a stray cat all my life, fighting for every scrap and morsel and constantly on the alert for danger? Who knew?

IVORY'S STORY

My box was lifted up and carried into a building. Even before we went through the door, my sensitive nose detected many foreign smells. There were cat smells and many dog smells. Each animal has its own distinctive odor and I knew there were a lot of different animals in this place.

The box was placed on a counter and soon a young man started questioning my transporter. I could tell he was young from his voice.

"What is in the box?"

"Can she breathe in there?"

"Let's take a look."

"How old is she?"

"How long have you had her?"

"Why are you surrendering her?" the young man inquired. Here I perked up and listened.

The man said, "Well, she didn't get along with our dog and she was always scratching my boys and the dog. It was a pain to clean her litter box. She climbed a tree and wouldn't come down. And well, we really don't need her."

The questions were answered quickly and with much dispassion. I was being surrendered! I would not be going back to my house or to my laundry room or to my former life, ever. My stomach twisted in a knot. Finally the tape was removed from the box and the lid was taken off. I blinked in the brightness of the lights and took a look around. I was in a large room with cages piled up, computers on the tables, charts, calendars, pictures and other paraphernalia taped to the walls, portable screens so I couldn't see behind them and just general clutter everywhere. But what really made an unfavorable impression on me was the noise. Dogs barking, whining, yipping. Cats crying, meowing. People laughing, talking loudly. The ruckus was almost more than I could stand. My ears hurt from all the commotion. I crouched down in the box, but without the protection of the lid, I was vulnerable to whatever was coming. The young man lifted me out of the box and turned me around. He had bright red hair and his hands were soft and caressing. He stroked me and this was a feeling I had not yet experienced in my young kitten life, living with the family who didn't want me. I was so shaken up by all the noise I was unable to move so I just let him hold me and turned my head into his chest.

He said, "Well, she's a pretty little thing."

No response from the older man who had begun to fill out the surrender paperwork. Finally, this part of the ordeal seemed to be over and he turned to leave.

He took one look at me over his shoulder and said, "Well, Kitty, have a nice life." And with that, he was out the door.

I was stunned. My life had just taken a turn for the worse and I was abandoned in a strange place, surrounded by a myriad of strange animals and strange people. I was homeless. A small sigh escaped from my thin lips.

The young man looked deep into my eyes and said, "It's alright. It's ok. We will take good care of you. You're better off here than with that man."

I wished I could have believed him.

"Now, we'll have to have you checked out to see if you are healthy. Let's put you into a cage for a while. It won't be bad."

He found one of the cleaner cages that had a soft towel on the bottom and gently lowered me into it. I peered out at him with wide eyes and then backed into a corner. I had never been in a cage before and I didn't like it. The steel bars were like a barrier to the outside world and it seemed so cold and impersonal and jail-like. "Clangk" was the sound made by the metal door locking me in. I was stuck in a steel trap. I couldn't get out and I wasn't sure I really wanted to get out. The noise was deafening. A cacophony of growls, hisses, yelps, and shouts assaulted my ears. Children were running and playing. I only heard their voices. I wanted to hide and I did nose myself under the towel somewhat so that I thought my body was hidden. This must be an animal shelter. That's *a n i m a l* shelter. I didn't think of myself as an animal, but now that's what I was ~ a caged one. Unable to escape or defend myself, I hid my face in the clean-smelling towel. People were coming and going through a revolving door close to my cage, but I didn't want to see them. I remained where I was for quite a while and after about two hours, the cage was lifted by someone and I was taken into a back room. I could sense the clinical feeling of this room even without seeing it. The smell was peculiar and I didn't care for it. The odor was sharp and somewhat unpleasant, like what I smelled when the woman doctored her son's finger after I scratched it. The room was quieter, but that didn't help my disposition. People seemed to be walking around with shoes that had rubber soles since I could hear them squeaking. The revolving door still swung open and shut, but I was taken away further from all the noise.

The person set my cage on a table. I stayed hidden. Presently, a woman's voice said, "So, this is Kitty. She has a pretty tail. Maybe we can see the rest of her."

Clangk went the door and I could sense a hand reaching inside the cage. The hand pulled me out by my scruff and set me on the cold metal table. I looked around. Bare walls, a sink with some instruments and a scale, an empty chair and the woman. She was wearing a white pinafore. Her dark hair was pulled back in a ponytail and she had kind eyes. She was looking intently at me and I stared back at her.

"You are very pretty indeed. Let's hope you won't be here very long. I want to weigh you."

She picked me up and put me on the scale. The scale said I weighed about three pounds. She took out her instrument and started to listen to my breathing. She opened my mouth and looked at my teeth and gums. She then took another instrument and stuck it in my ears. I seemed to be getting a clean bill of health. She lifted my tail and ran her fingers through my fur. She felt my ribs. Then she found some claw clippers and took hold of my right paw and clipped my sharp little kitten nails. It didn't hurt, but I didn't like it. She did the same with my left paw and the back ones.

"You are almost good to go, Kitty. Let's give you your kitten vaccinations."

She pulled out a syringe filled with some potion and quickly stuck it in my hind leg. It stung a bit but I didn't complain. Then she took my scruff and held my head back while I had to inhale some type of liquid drops. I sneezed and sniffled. She stroked me several times and put me back in the cage. I hid in the back. The lady left the room. So went my first examination by a vet.

The cage was confining but at least I didn't feel exposed. I continued to hide under the towel. Soon, a young woman opened the door to the room and lifted me in my cage. I didn't want to see where I was being taken. The loud noises became louder and I could tell I was now in the room with dogs and cats and who knows what else. The door to my cage opened and another strange hand snaked in and picked me up. The hand smelled doggy and this was frightening. Surely they wouldn't put me in a cage with a dog? No, I was placed in my own cage with another clean towel. I shriveled up in the back and peered out at my new world. This was a large room with cages everywhere. Cages on shelves, cages on the floor, cages on cages. Most cages were occupied by a single cat or dog. I figured that they weren't married either. Many cats were napping. Napping! How could they ignore all the din and commotion and actually sleep? Several dogs were barking and some were just watching the parade of people and animals. There were old cats, young cats, and a few kittens they had grouped together in cages. I assumed these kittens were from the same litters. Clowders of felines, they were. The cats were long haired, short haired and there was even one with no fur. The cat was naked!

The dogs had larger cages, depending on their size. Some dogs looked expectantly at the people milling around. Some were hyper, bouncing around in their cages. Some seemed to be from another planet, barking at some dog satellite, only known to dogs. How undisciplined they seemed. Why bark? To call attention to oneself? If so, it didn't seem to be working. The people seemed to be more interested in talking to each other than in the animals. I was very hungry and thirsty. I hoped that it would be feeding time at the OK Corral soon since it had been many hours since I had eaten. I really needed some water because my mouth was so dry. I noticed that there were water dishes in the other cages and there were small litter boxes in the cats' cages.

I saw a paw next door reach out through the bars. The paw was white and the pads were pink. The paws gripped the bars and then searched the air as if trying to grab something. I decided to take a chance and speak.

"Who are you?" I inquired.

"My name is Ivory. You're new here, aren't you?" the soft voice answered.

"Yeah I was dumped here a few hours ago."

"Well, you won't be in this room very long, I hope," she said.

"I'm scared. The noise is deafening."

Ivory said, "You'll get used to it after a while."

"Let me see you." I scooted up close to the bars so I could see my neighbor.

A pretty white face peered over at me from the adjoining cage. She had a pink nose and large jade green eyes. She was a good sized cat and I could tell she was pure white with no other markings on her. Her short fur looked soft and well-groomed.

"Why are you here?" I asked.

"My owners left me because they were moving into an apartment and they couldn't keep a cat there. I had been with them for years and they had to give me up. Now, who knows what will happen to me."

"I hate it here," I told her.

She exclaimed, "You are just a kitten! You're too young to hate anything. How did you come to this place?" I told her briefly about what had happened and the people who were in my life for several months. I didn't go into the particulars about how I had suffered and been neglected in favor of a dog. This was really the first cat conversation I ever had besides the few little kitten ones I engaged in with my brothers and sisters when I was very young. It was pleasant to talk to another cat. Ivory's face was animated and very expressive, like all cats' faces. She seemed interested in my story and listened without interruption.

She wanted to know what my name was and I told her, "Kitty." She said, "There are probably several 'Kittys' here so they may rename you." I thought that would be a good idea.

I asked, "When will they give me something to eat and drink? It's been so long since I've eaten."

She answered, "Well, dinner time is usually around 5:00 or 6:00 so it shouldn't be too long now. This room is really a holding room until they decide what to do with you. I've been here before, but it's been a long time. They usually separate the dogs from the cats, but you'll still be able to hear the barking through the walls. Some dogs bark all night long. Some bark all throughout the day, so there's really no respite from it. They put the cats that need socializing in a small room. These are the wild cats, the feral ones. They don't have much chance of being adopted unless they calm down and behave the way people want. Many of them do finally come around and are able to be handled and some even are friendly toward people. A few never will make good pets. I'm not sure what happens to them."

I digested this bit of information and licked my paws. The day had been a sensory overload and I was tired. I settled down in the back corner and laid my head on my paw. I couldn't sleep but I could rest.

After a while, the noise increased and the smells of food awakened my senses. I stood up and saw most of the dogs were looking at the door, through which a girl brought a tray of canned and dry food. A frenzy of barking ensued. She started feeding the dogs first, opening each cage door and plopping a large amount of both types of food in the bowls. The dogs gulped and ate like pigs. One or two mouthfuls and the food was gone. How uncouth!

Finally she came around to Ivory's cage. I saw Ivory rub up against the bars and back off when the girl opened the door. The food smelled ok. She came to my cage and put in a small dish of water and some cat food in another dish. I waited until she had locked the cage door and then I ate and drank quickly but daintily. It was then time for me to wash. My pink tongue was rough against my fur and the feeling was almost like a massage. Most of the other cats were washing too. I stayed in the back of the cage until Ivory said, "Do you feel better now?" I said I did. She urged me to try to get some rest.

I was really exhausted. It had been such a long day, starting out with me high up in the tree. There was just too much for me to process in one day. And this was just the beginning...

LIFE AT THE SHELTER

The next morning I was awakened early by the dogs barking. Would they ever shut up? Even during the night, I could hear them constantly barking. I felt like I didn't get enough sleep, but I was hoping for a catnap later. I heard Ivory moving around in her cage.

"Ivory? Are you awake?"

"Yes but just barely. I haven't really had a good night's sleep since I came here."

"What do you do all day?"

"Nothing, really. They make us stay in the cage for most of the day so I try to sleep, but the dogs keep me awake."

"Do they ever let you out of the cage?" I asked.

"Sometimes there are people who come in to play with the dogs and cats and then they put us in the room where the toys are. And if we're lucky, we might be moved into an area that's farther away from the dogs and a bit quieter."

Anything would be quieter than this place, I thought.

I stretched and looked out at the other animals in the room. There were more cats than dogs, but you wouldn't know it from the noise. I saw a big tomcat staring at me. He was a tuxedo cat, with white markings on his chest and white paws, but the rest of his coloring was black. His eyes glittered and he narrowed them as he stared. I looked away. I wouldn't want to go into the playroom with him or any of the other cats. I wasn't used to other cats. I only had one friend here so far. In fact, Ivory was the only friend I had ever had since I left my brothers and sisters.

Another cat was making a big ruckus, banging around in the cage, rattling the bars and making the cage shake. The cat had vivid tabby markings that were mostly gray and black. I could see this was a feral cat and I felt sorry for him. This cat was wild and terrified and this was probably the first time he had ever been confined. The cat's nose was bleeding from hitting it against the bars. You would think they could have provided a padded cage for the wild ones so they wouldn't hurt themselves.

How did all these cats get here? Surely they weren't all surrendered like Ivory and I had been. Maybe someone had trapped them and brought them in. Maybe an animal control officer had found them. But one thing I knew for sure was that they didn't just walk in of their own accord off the street. Not one would have chosen to be penned up in a small cage. I supposed that in some ways a cage was better than being on the street. Here at least they fed you and it was protected from the elements. But what sort of life was this? Two feet by three feet of cold metal with no chance of escape. This wasn't a home; this was merely a holding place until someone adopted you. Hopefully the adoptions would come quickly.

I knew that kittens had a much better chance of being adopted than the older cats did. Everyone wants a cute playful kitten, but not many people want a grown cat. Older cats make great pets but people go for the little ones.

A routine was established. We were fed twice a day and our litter boxes were cleaned every other day. Ivory and I became friends and if it wasn't for her, I would have been bored to tears. That is, if cats could cry tears. She had lived with her people for years and as they became older, they decided they had to move to a smaller place. Unfortunately for Ivory, the place they chose wasn't pet-friendly. The day before they moved, Ivory was packed into her carrying cage and brought to the shelter. It was a very sad day for Ivory and her people. Ivory's whole life had been upended and so had her peoples' lives. Since arriving at the shelter, she had been in the cage for a while, hoping she would be moved into another area, away from the barking dogs and the constant activity. That hadn't happened yet. There were so many cats living at the shelter, the premium spots were already taken.

One day, we were both removed from our cages and carried into a special room only for cats. It was relatively quiet in there and in the room were about 10 other cats. There were cat trees for climbing and scratching, cat toys, most of which I had never known about, a dish with some water, a couch and two people. The people were there to play with us. This was a new experience for me, as I never had the chance to play when I lived with my family. A woman held a laser pointer and the light moved across the floor, like a small red bug. This was enticing! A few cats chased it and I waited for the light to come over my way. When the red light swooped past me, I reached out a paw to touch it, but it was gone in a flash. I then saw the light climb up the wall and I ran over to it and jumped up to catch it, but again, it disappeared. I knew it was only a laser, but I really loved playing with it. A few small catnip mice were on the floor so I batted one of them around for a while. It was fun to pick it up in my mouth and pretend it was a real mouse.

As I was carrying it, I saw the big black and white tomcat moving my way. He was eyeing me and again, he scared me. He wanted my mouse! I ran behind the couch with it and he followed me. I turned and looked at him and snarled. Snarled! I didn't know I could do that. He puffed out his fur and gave me a look that said, "Give me the mouse!" I growled and retreated further behind the couch. Just then, the woman moved the couch away from the wall and told the tom to back off. He backed up from the space and walked over to one of the cat trees where he stretched out.

I took my mouse into the play area and continued to bat it around. It smelled faintly of catnip. Most of those catnip mice are stuffed with old catnip and aren't very potent. I would have liked some freshly picked catnip, but no one cared about my wishes.

The woman came over and picked me up and held me on her lap. I didn't really mind this and she probably thought she was socializing me. I didn't need socializing, but I let her think she was doing me a favor.

"Kitty! You are a very pretty little thing," she said to me. I already knew this.

"I wish I could take you home with me, but I already have two cats at home." I thought, "Only two?" I was sure many other people had more than two cats in their homes.

LINDA C MARCHMAN

Ivory was also in the playroom with me. She wasn't as active as I was and she had found a perch on a cat tree several feet above the floor where she watched the action below. She called me over and told me to climb up to her perch, which I did. It felt good to be able to climb, since my only real experience with climbing had been on the tree at my previous home. I settled in beside her and she licked the back and top of my head where I wasn't able to reach. I moved closer to her and her body heat warmed me. I felt a sense of contentment. I purred. I could have stayed in the playroom for a long time, but then it was time to go back to the cage. As I was being carried out, the black tom gave me a warning look. I hadn't done anything to him; I was just a little kitten.

Time passed. I became somewhat passive, in that my days were spent mostly in my cage, chatting with Ivory or observing the action in the room. Then, what we thought was a wonderful change happened. Ivory and I, along with some other cats were moved out of the room where the dogs were into a quieter part of the building. There were only cats in this area and I was finally able to catch some undisturbed catnaps and sleep during the night. This was what they called, "The Adoption Room" where prospective adopters could walk through and view the waiting adoptees. There were some chairs in the middle of the room and there were many other cages that held cats. We were still confined to our cages, but once a day a volunteer, who was usually a woman, came by and took us out of our cages and handled us and played with us. I assumed she was trying to get us ready to live with a new family. I didn't mind this, as it gave me a change of routine for a while.

Every day, people would come in the room and walk slowly by our cages, checking us out. There were all types of people. Some had babies or little children and I didn't think it would have been a good idea to adopt a cat or especially a kitten when one had young children to cope with. The children don't know their own strength and that can be hazardous for us. There were couples who were looking for their first pet and examined us carefully. I hoped to pass inspection so I came forward in my cage so they could see my black, orange, and white markings.

The first person who wanted to see me up close asked the attendant to take me out of the cage. I was removed and taken to a chair so the prospect could watch me. The potential adopter was a young man, in his early twenties. He smelled like he had been smoking cigarettes, but he was fairly gentle with me. His beard tickled my face and I swatted at him with my claws sheathed. He laughed and tickled my chin. He put me down on the floor and I ran under the chair and peeked out at him.

"I might consider you, but I have to look at some other cats first," he stated as he scooped me up and placed me in my cage. I thought that it might not be too bad to live with this man. I watched him as he passed over Ivory and several others. As he came to the end of the row, a long-haired pumpkin- colored cat reached out to him through the bars.

"Ah ha! Do you want to go home with me?" he asked the cat. Pumpkin Face responded by continuing to try to grab the man. He was aggressive about it, I thought, but the man didn't seem to mind. The man had Pumpkin Face taken out of the cage and they seemed to bond right away. Pumpkin Face clung to the man and nuzzled his beard.

"This is the one I want," the man told the attendant.

"Wonderful! Let's go up front so you can fill out the paperwork."

And that was how Pumpkin Face found a home. I decided I might need to be a little more forward in my approach to potential care-givers. This really wasn't my style, but I didn't want to spend the rest of my life at the animal shelter.

I asked Ivory, "How long do you think it will take before we're adopted?"

"Well, it depends. The right person has to come along and notice you. You have to catch that person's attention. If you think that one is for you, make some noise. Talk to them. Interact with them. Get yourself noticed. Look cute. You'll learn what to do. It just might work out to your advantage."

Ok, so I needed to practice my meows. I needed to present myself so I was attractive to people. I started meowing.

Ivory said, "What wrong with you?"

"I'm just practicing."

"Practicing what? Listening to your own voice?"

"No, I was working on my 'come hither' meows."

"Ha ha. Just try being yourself instead."

"Well, who else could I be?" This conversation wasn't going anywhere so I sat back and tried to relax. More people came through the room that day but none really appealed to me so I didn't make an effort to attract them. I stayed in the back of the cage until it was dinner time.

Several days went by and then it turned into a week. There was a constant parade of people who came to see the cats. I felt like I was in a zoo, caged and on display. A few people actually adopted cats, but the majority did not. There seemed to be a fee involved when someone wanted to take a cat home and I guess many people did not have the money to pay. I didn't know if this was good or bad. If they couldn't pay the fee, maybe they couldn't provide the essentials for their new pet. Of course, they may be financially able to pay the fee, but emotionally wouldn't provide a good home for their new cat. It was all a gamble and at stake were our lives.

One day, a mother and her two small children came in. The mother looked harried as she tried to shepherd her children and corral them. The little ones looked to be about 2 or 3 years old. They immediately spotted Ivory and the children came running over to her cage. They started poking their fingers through the bars and trying to grab Ivory's fur. I knew Ivory wouldn't stand for this treatment for very long. I heard Ivory hiss at them and emit a low growl which scared them. The mother yanked the kids' arms away from the cage and told them not to touch the cage or the cats. Not heeding her words, they looked my way and started rattling the bars on my cage. This scared me and I retreated to the back.

"Cat! Cat!" they screamed.

"Leave the cat alone!" The mother was getting angry.

"Would you like to see Kitty?" asked the volunteer.

No! Please don't take me out! Please no!

"Well, I guess it wouldn't hurt." The mother was looking doubtful and I was becoming more frightened every second.

Ivory whispered, "Scratch them if you need to." I had claws and even though they had been trimmed they could still hurt someone, but I didn't want to use them unless it was necessary.

I was picked up and put on the tile floor close to the children. They both squealed and started chasing me. I was terrified. I tried to hide under a chair, but they crawled under it after me. I ran to the other side of the room and they followed. The volunteer suddenly left the room and it was just me, the mother and her kids, and all the other cats in the cages watching.

The mother said, "Don't chase the kitty. You'll scare her." The children continued to run after me. The mother was looking at some of the other cats in the cages and not paying attention to her two little tormenters. I tried to wedge myself behind a door, but they just moved the door and I was exposed and cornered. One child started jumping up and down excitedly and the other one moved closer to me. A grubby little hand grabbed my tail and pulled it. It hurt! I tried to extract my tail from his hand and it wouldn't budge. The kid didn't know his own strength, but I knew mine and now was the time to use it. I quickly reached out with one paw with all claws fully extended and scratched the hand that held my tail.

"Ooowww! Waahh!" cried the child. He began to yell and carry on like he had been bitten by a tiger and held his bleeding hand so a few drops of blood dripped on the floor. The other child stood looking stupidly at him. The mother came running over to examine the hand.

"Well, what did you expect when you kept chasing the kitty? What did I tell you?"

The volunteer must have heard all the commotion and reappeared. She took in the scene and quickly picked me up and set me back in my cage.

Ivory said, "Good for you."

I was so exhausted, I hid under the towel in my cage. I didn't want to see these people anymore. They didn't need a cat in their home. I just wanted to be left alone.

The child continued to scream and the mother took out a tissue to wipe the blood away and pressed it on the scratch. The screams upset the other cats and some tried to hide in their cages. The volunteer suggested that the family go into another room to calm down. Luckily they took her advice. I survived this time.

Every day, people would come in the adoption room browsing for potential cat housemates. A few would be chosen, but there were always many more who weren't. At night, when the lights were out, the cats would talk about which ones were adopted that day. We knew that good homes were few and far between. Every few days, a few more new cats would be brought in and the cages were crammed together like so many sardines in a tin can. I saw an old gray tabby cat taken out one day and he never returned. He hadn't been adopted so I didn't want to think about what happened to him. He never moved around his cage much and he always looked weak and sickly. No one ever gave him a second look and I felt sorry for him. People don't adopt cats that have problems or are less than desirable in their eyes.

Ivory and I became good friends. I started hoping that we would be adopted together, but I knew that probably wouldn't happen. She told me stories about when she lived with her family and how good they were to her. The people were older and they gave her a good home. She would sit on their laps and purr and they would stroke her. She was a contented cat and they were content having her live with them. She was an indoor cat and consequently always very healthy. She had a window seat where she could watch the birds and squirrels outside. The people even had a screened porch where Ivory could go when the weather permitted. The house had finally become too much for them to take care of, so they had to decide what to do and where to go. Unfortunately for Ivory they chose a place to move that didn't allow cats or other pets. Over the course of several weeks, there was a lot of packing of boxes with clothes and possessions. Ivory loved the empty boxes and played in them, pretending that they were cat caves. Gradually she came to realize that she wouldn't be going with the people. What would happen to her? The children were all grown and living in other places. It wouldn't be convenient for one of them to give her a home. Since the people took such good care of her, Ivory knew they wouldn't just turn her out to live on her own. Maybe they would take her back to the shelter. She had been in the shelter years before when she was young and she didn't relish the thought of going through the experience again. Of course, when she was younger, she was more adoptable, too. Now, she had some age on her and it would be harder to find a good home. Ivory loved these people and she knew they loved her. It was hard to think about not being with them for the rest of her years.

It was a sad time on the day before the movers came. Early in the morning, Ivory had a good breakfast. They even fed her some bacon, which she gobbled down. The people talked soothingly to her, but she could tell they were trying to hold back their tears. Her cage was brought out. The woman and the man each took turns holding her and telling her everything would be all right. Ivory didn't know whether they meant this for her or for themselves. She clung to their necks and they were both sobbing. It was a terrible and heartrending time for everyone. Finally it was time to go. The cage was placed in the car and she was driven to the shelter where she was surrendered. The story that continued was basically the same as mine from then on, except Ivory was heartbroken as she was left in the care of the shelter employees. The people never came back to visit her. She had now been living in the shelter for a while. I hoped that she would be able to find a good home, one in which she could live a peaceful life, free from anxiety. I guess that's what all the other shelter inmates wanted too.

One evening, the attendant brought the dinner tray in the room. She moved around the room, filling everyone's bowls and freshening their water. When she came to me, she said, "Sorry, Kitty, no food for you to-night." I was left standing there looking quizzically at her. She didn't offer any explanation.

When everyone else was eating, I asked Ivory, "Why don't I get to eat?"

"Well, I'm not sure, but it may be because they plan to spay you tomorrow."

Spay me? Wasn't I too young for this?

"Ivory, have you been spayed?" I inquired.

"Yes, but it was many years ago. I was taken to a vet's office and given some anesthesia. I don't remember anything else except when I woke up, I was in pain. I felt like a part of me was missing, which it was. My lower parts hurt for a while and they released me back home the next day. My people took care of me and kept me in a small room where I couldn't jump up on any furniture. This was to keep my stitches from coming apart. Gradually I healed and from then on, I felt fine. I wasn't ever able to have kittens, but that was ok with me."

No kittens for me. Ever. I really hadn't given it much thought, but it may have been a good thing since I didn't have a husband or even a male cat friend. I didn't want one, either. I didn't know what was in store for me, but I began to mentally prepare myself. I was hungry that night and didn't sleep well, thinking about all the possible outcomes of my upcoming surgery, if that was going to happen.

The next morning I again didn't get any breakfast when the attendant arrived with the food tray. I looked longingly at Ivory's cat food as she munched away. Presently, a white-clad woman came in the room and walked over to my cage. She checked the identification tag to make sure I was the same "Kitty" she was looking for and took me out. I said goodbye to Ivory. Cradled in her arm, she took me into a room that smelled like a hospital. Disinfectant smells were pungent and I tried not to breathe deeply. I was put into another cage and I waited for what seemed like hours, but was probably only minutes. Finally, the same vet who checked me in when I came to the shelter opened the door. She had some serious-looking equipment with her. Another white-coated vet tech was with her. They both started setting up the equipment while I watched.

"Kitty, very soon you'll be asleep and won't know what's happened. You'll wake up and you'll be sore for a few days and we'll give you some pain medicine which will help. Now, we're going to shave your arm so we can insert the IV."

They both removed me from the cage. I tried to grab the bars, but they were insistent on getting me out. The tech held me on the table with one hand and used the electric shaver with the other hand to shave the fur off my arm. Oh, I didn't like this one bit. I wanted to go back to my cage and have it be an ordinary day, but it was not to be. My eyes must have shown my fear because both women kept talking to me in soothing voices reassuring me that I'd be ok.

Then came the scary part. Using a needle, they inserted it into my vein. The needle's prick startled me and I tried to withdraw my paw but the effort was useless. Oh, let me live through this, I prayed. Soon, I began to feel sleepy and then I must have fallen asleep. I didn't know how long I was out, but when I woke up I was very groggy. My head felt strange and I was dizzy. I looked around and noticed I was in another room which was quiet and warm. I glanced down at my tummy and saw it also had been shaved and it now had some tiny staples in it. This is what Ivory had warned me about. I had been spayed but most importantly I was still alive. I rested my head on the paw that was not shaved, hoping the effects of the anesthesia would wear off soon. I thought that things were always happening to me in my short life that I had no control over. People had been making decisions that affected me and I was just a pawn. As I went back to sleep I thought that I would like to change that.

When I next woke up, I felt sick. Luckily I hadn't had anything to eat recently. My underparts were sore and I wanted to lick that area, but someone had placed a plastic collar around my neck so it was impossible to lick myself. The collar was awkward and chafed my neck. It was made of hard plastic and both sides were connected with some Velcro. I pawed at it, but it was fastened securely so I had to wear it. My neck hurt from being in an uncomfortable position for so long. Uggghh. They had taped my arm where the IV had been. I tried to pull the tape off without success. The adhesive pulled at my skin. I reached out to the bars and started rattling them. No one came. I settled back down in the cage and waited.

After a while, I thought I'd try out my newly-practiced meows. "Let meeeoouuut!" I called. Rattling the bars again, I repeated my plea. Silence. As I became more aware of my surroundings, I noticed there were a few other cages in the room containing cats. Most of these cats were ones I had seen in the adoption room, but with whom I wasn't acquainted. Some of the cats were watching me as I banged on the cage but most were ignoring me. These may have been cats who were spayed or neutered recently. A dark striped tabby across from me sat up and looked straight at me.

"Nice collar," he stated. I knew he was making fun of me so I shrugged off his remark.

"Are you going to a Renaissance fashion show?" he continued. "I've seen better looking lampshades."

"Why are you in here?" I asked him.

"Well, they decided I needed to be neutered, so I'll be spending the night here."

"What's your name?"

"Romeo." he replied.

I couldn't help but snicker. "Looks like you'll have to get them to change that now."

He looked down and didn't meet my eyes.

"Sorry, I didn't mean to offend you."

"I'm sorry I made fun of your collar. What's your name?" he asked.

"Kitty. I wish someone would change my name."

"Whoever adopts you may change it."

"I sure hope that's soon." My collar was uncomfortable as I tried to move around the cage. I stumbled and lay back down.

"You're very pretty and shouldn't be here very long at the shelter. The plain looking cats are the ones who spend a lot of time here. People want pretty cats, but many of us are older and not so cute anymore."

I felt bad for the plain ones and the not so cute ones. They needed a home as much as everyone else. I was very tired so I told Romeo that I was going to take a nap. It felt like my head was underwater as I rested and soon I fell asleep.

In the morning, I was put back into my cage beside Ivory. The collar was like a large plastic visor around my neck. I pawed and scraped at it and it chafed my neck. I knew it was for my own protection so I wouldn't pull out my staples, but it was worse than the staples themselves. And now, the pain medicine was beginning to wear off and I could feel the staples as they held my skin together. This wasn't fun. How much longer did I have to wear this stupid collar? Collars are for dogs. I looked around for Romeo but didn't see him.

Ivory was just waking up and she asked me if I was okay. I told her that I was hurting but at least I wasn't as woozy as I was the day before. I was also beginning to feel hungry.

"Have they brought breakfast yet?" I asked her.

"Yes, about an hour ago."

"I hope they don't forget about me."

Presently, a vet tech came in and walked up to my cage. She looked me over and said, "Kitty, I'm going to give you more pain medicine so you'll be more comfortable today." With that, she pried open my mouth and squirted some medicine in my cheek. It tasted terrible. I wondered why medicines didn't come in bird or mouse flavors. The tech then changed my water, but didn't put any food in my dish. It looked like I was going to go hungry again. I reached out my paw to her but she just patted me on the head and closed the cage door.

After an hour or so, I started to feel lightheaded again. It was difficult standing up and I decided to sleep as much as I could while I was recuperating. I ignored the other cats in the cages who were making snide comments about my collar and I lay down as best as I could. The big tuxedo cat was staring at me and I knew that he would love to be out of his cage to torment me or worse.

I slept through most of the day and even the visitors didn't bother me. There must have been a sign on my cage telling the people to leave me alone. I did remember later that someone came in and asked to look at Ivory. I was so sleepy that I didn't pay much attention, but when I woke up the next time, Ivory was gone.

"Ivory?" I asked groggily. "Ivory, are you there?" No answer.

I heard one of the other cats saying that Ivory was gone.

"Where did she go?" I called out, slurring my words.

Someone answered, "They took her away earlier and we haven't seen her since."

I started to panic. My only friend was gone. What would I do without Ivory? Oh, what had happened while I was asleep? I grabbed the bars and shook them but no one paid attention.

"Meooooww!" I cried pitifully. I was feeling not only bad physically, but now I was emotionally distraught.

"Ivorrryy!!"

There was nothing I could do but keep hoping that Ivory would come back. If she had been adopted, I'd never see her again. It would be a good thing for her to have a home, but I was feeling selfish and concerned that I would wither away without her friendship and sweet personality to cheer me up. I had grown to love Ivory and I think she felt the same about me. I could hear the black and white tuxedo cat laughing at me. He definitely had a cattitude. I was purely dejected. I faced the back of my cage, curled up into a furry ball and whimpered.

CHAINSAW MAN

The tree trunk offered partial shelter and I took advantage of the opportunity to rest. My paw was still throbbing so I licked it and hoped this would soothe it. I looked over at the cows, contentedly munching on some hay that someone had provided. Cows didn't seem to be very picky in what they ate. I thought hay would be somewhat tasteless, but they ate large portions and chewed it thoroughly. A low bellow sounded from the other side of a small hill. The cows looked up at the sound and a white truck rumbled over the hill. There were a few young, frisky calves chasing each other around the pasture but they stopped when they saw the truck pull up. The mother cows kept an eye on the little ones and the truck. A large man emerged from the driver's side, wearing a red plaid flannel shirt and baggy jeans. Walking toward the back of the truck, he removed a chainsaw from the truck bed. He lowered the tailgate and started checking the saw. When he tried to start it, the cows perked up again. After several tries, the saw started with a very loud grinding noise and the cows began a mini-stampede the other way. I was very wary of this stranger and his loud machine. Soon, he started walking toward the old fallen tree and toward my hideout. This was disturbing, so I hauled myself out and skittered away to hide behind another tree at a safe distance. I peeked out and in my peripheral vision, I saw a pale orange cat scoot up a tree. So, there were other cats in these woods, not just the kittens I saw earlier.

Climbing over fallen limbs and branches, the man began sawing up the medium sized limbs that were lying on the ground. He would saw one piece and saw another about the same length. Oh, the sound of the saw was hurting my ears! I figured that I had better run while I still could. When the man's back was toward me, I scampered up a tree and hid on a lower branch. I was good at climbing trees by this time - I had a lot of practice. I could gaze at the man, but he couldn't see me. After sawing a number of wood chunks, he turned off the saw and put it on the ground. He walked back to the truck and backed it close to the newly- sawn logs and started throwing the wood into the bed of the truck. I could tell that this was hard work for him because he was wiping his face and breathing heavily. He stopped after a while and sat down on what was left of the tree trunk. He actually hadn't sawed up too much of my hiding place and I was happy about that. After a while, he got up and started his job of throwing the wood pieces into the truck again. The truck was about half full when all of a sudden, the man swayed dizzily and dropped to the ground! It looked like he had knocked himself out by falling and he wasn't moving. Sprawled out, with his flannel shirt missing a button and his boots muddy from the damp ground, the man looked like he was taking a nap. I knew that he was alive because I could see him breathing, but his breath was labored and shallow. He lay motionless on the leaf-strewn ground.

ROMEO'S STORY

Later, when it was getting dark, I saw someone carry a bundle into the room. The lights had been dimmed but my eyes were keen and the bundle looked like it was white. The person walked closer to me and then I saw that Ivory was in her hands! Ivory was put back into her cage and there was silence.

"Ivory! Where have you been? I've been so worried about you."

Ivory was slow in answering, "They took me into the playroom to see if I would play. They threw balls at me and I tried to run away but there wasn't any place to hide. They were aggressive and they scared me. There weren't any supervisors in the room and I couldn't defend myself since I don't have any claws. They really were looking for a younger cat and I just didn't fit the bill. I think the supervisor forgot about me and just left me in the cage after the people had gone. Oh, I'll never be adopted! I'll probably have to live my whole life in this cage!"

I felt so bad for poor Ivory. I said, "Oh, no you won't. Those people just weren't a good match for you. You'll see, sometime the right person will come along and will fall in love with you."

"I'm just an old white cat." Ivory responded. "I used to be young and pretty and I had a good home. Now, look at me. No claws and overweight."

"You're beautiful!" I cried. "White cats are rare. You have beautiful eyes and you're intelligent and kind. You have me for a friend."

She didn't say anything so I let her rest. I wasn't feeling so good myself. The pain medicine made me drowsy.

Gradually as a few days went by, I began to feel better. I especially felt better the day the e-collar was removed. I could turn my head again and wash myself. I attended to my stitches and I could feel that I was healing. Spaying wasn't so bad. At least I'd never have to worry about kittens and whether I could take care of them. Ivory and I talked throughout the days to relieve the boredom. We both liked it when we were allowed into the playroom where we had some freedom and we could choose what to do. There were tunnels to run through and cat trees to climb. A few windows had perches where we could look outside. There wasn't much to look at outdoors but the parking lot, but at least it was a change of scenery. We were provided with a lot of good toys including catnip mice, marbles, ropes to chase, and many others that appeal to cats. I liked it when one of the attendants would turn on the laser pointer. That always attracted many of the other cats in the room. We'd follow the red light and pounce on it. It was fun to play with and good exercise as well. The playroom was my favorite place in the shelter. The only time I didn't like it was when they allowed the black and white tuxedo cat in when I was there. He would watch me and sometimes act like he wanted to attack me. His eyes would narrow and were like glittering black diamonds as he stared at me. I couldn't understand why he acted this way. Luckily, the volunteer was usually in the room so that kept him in check. Why do some cats act out and some are pussycats? Each one of us has a different personality, just like people. A lot depends on their background and whether they've had good experiences in their lives or not. A cat that has been handled roughly and ignored is bound to have a complex. "Tux" must have had a bad kittenhood.

Sometimes Romeo would be in the room with me. We got along well together. Romeo was very active and he would run around the room working off some of his energy, or more appropriately, "playing" off his energy. He was friendly with the other cats and he liked people. He told me a little bit about his background. Romeo was born in a barn, out in the country. There were all kinds of animals around, but his mother kept him and his sister hidden in a corner most of the time. Romeo's mother was a pretty gray and white striped cat with short, dense fur. Juliet, his sister, looked much like his mother and one could tell that she would grow up to be a stunning adult cat. She was a bit unusual because she was a polydactyl, with an extra toe on each front paw.

A horse would come in to eat some hay and sleep in the stall at night. At first the horse scared Romeo and his sister, but after a while they got used to him. The horse was tame and didn't bother the kittens. A man would lead the horse in and pen him in his stall. The man knew the kittens were also in the barn, but he didn't touch them or pay much attention to them. Romeo and Juliet were interested in the man. They weren't skittish, so sometimes they would follow the man out of the barn. Being curious, they would explore the immediate surroundings before scampering back to the confines of the barn when their mother called. As they looked around outside, they could see farm implements and fields of grass. A vegetable garden was off to one side, fenced in to keep out the deer. A house was in the distance and that was where the man usually went after securing his horse in the stall. The kittens had an urge to explore further, but mama kept them in check. She hunted and brought back tidbits for her kittens.

The barn offered protection and a sanctuary from the elements so it was the ideal place for the cats. A bed made out of hay was in a corner for the kittens and it was a dry and soft place for catnapping.

One day, when the summer sun was hot early in the morning, the man came into the barn and led his horse out of the stall. Romeo and Juliet could see the horse trotting around in a circle, getting some exercise. The kittens ventured outside and started playing in the grass, looking for grasshoppers to eat and butterflies to chase. They were running and chasing each other and soon they were farther from the barn than they had ever been. The grass was tall and they played hide and seek in it. No one could see them and they couldn't see where they were. In the course of their play, they found themselves close to a wooded area. The area was different from anything they had ever seen, and being kittens with a high curiosity level, they moved closer to the trees to explore some new territory. The woods offered some protection from the harsh sun and it was cooler underneath the trees. They carefully padded along until they came upon an old well, lined with moss-covered rocks. They could hear a faint sound of an underground spring close by, but having had no experience with wells, they both wanted to investigate it. Romeo put both his paws on a rock and peered down the hole. Juliet, the more cautious one, stayed close to the edge, but on the floor of the woods. All of a

sudden, the old rock that Romeo was standing on gave
way and he tumbled down several feet. He could hear
the rock rolling further down the shaft then and striking other rocks. The rock landed at the bottom with a
splash and Romeo tried scrabbling back up the other
stones to safety. It was no use. The rocks were slippery
and his tentative hold on them faltered. Romeo was
very frightened and he had a wild look in his eyes as
he began to slide downward toward the bottom of the
well. He cried out to Juliet, but there was nothing she
could do to help him. As he tried to regain a hold on
a rock, he glanced down and saw the water below. He
panicked and slid down a few more feet. He could look
up and see his sister and the sunlight, but looking down
it was all black. His back paw found a slight foothold in
a crevasse and he managed to balance precariously on
it while gripping the side of another slippery stone with
his front paws. His little body was bruised from striking
the rocks and he was in pain. He cried again to Juliet
as he clung to the side of the well.

"Help me! Help meeeeowwt, Juliet!"

It was cool down in the well and as he looked up
again, he didn't see Juliet anymore. His keen kitten
ears could pick up the sound of her little mewing, faint
and far away. He hoped that someone would rescue
him soon or he would drown in the dark well.

After what seemed like an eternity, he could hear
the sound of his mama anxiously calling for him. He

was getting weaker, trying to hold on to the rocks and he could only manage a small whimper as his claws tried to dig into the hard surface of the rock.

Mama could see him hanging on down in the well, but she didn't know what to do. She ran back and forth frantically and called and called little Romeo. Finally she also disappeared. Romeo knew she wouldn't abandon him, but his hopes were growing dimmer each minute.

Another eternity elapsed and when he looked up again, he could see the man who lived in the house squinting and looking down the well at him. It appeared the man was considering climbing down to rescue him and then thought again. He could then hear the sound of the man running away. Oh, what next? Romeo despaired. The water seemed to get closer to him, but maybe it was just his imagination. He tried not to think of what might happen if his grip failed. The water would be cold and deep. He didn't know how to swim or how to survive in water. He would sink and that would be the end of his short kitten life. He hadn't even reached the age of one year and he would be gone forever.

The man finally returned and had hooked up a basket to the end of a long and sturdy rope. He lowered the basket into the well slowly. Romeo could see the basket coming toward him and he knew it was his lifesaver. Now, if he could avoid being knocked into the water by the basket, he might have a chance. The basket came closer. It banged on the sides of the well. Luckily Romeo was a small cat and the basket wasn't too big. The basket hovered just above his head and inched down so it was parallel to him. The man was very careful handling the basket because he knew the danger it posed. The question remained of how Romeo was going to haul himself into the basket that was hanging by a rope and swinging back and forth.

Romeo could hear the man saying, "Come on, you can do it. Just put your paw in it and grab the basket. Be careful. I'll hold it steady."

Romeo was in a quandary. He had to hold on to his position on the slippery rock and at the same time try to swing himself over into the basket. He knew he only had one chance to do this. If he missed, he would fall the rest of the way down into the well with no chance of rescue. He was cold and losing his grip on the rock. The basket was lowered a few more inches. As it came closer, Romeo put out a tentative paw and hooked the basket top to bring it near his feet. Then, he made a sudden move and he was hanging halfway out of the basket with his back half out and front half in. He pulled the rest of his little furry body into the basket and looked up. The man started hauling the kitten and basket out of the well to safety. The man had saved Romeo's life and he was very grateful. At the top of the well, Mama and Juliet were waiting. Romeo rubbed up against his sister and mother and then rubbed against the man's ankles. The man picked up Romeo and tucked him into his arm. The cats followed as the man returned to the house.

Romeo had never been in a house before and it was all very strange and confining. He was put on the floor and the man gave him some milk, which Romeo lapped up greedily. He was so happy to be alive and out of the well. The man stroked his back and Romeo began to purr. Soon, the little cat began to feel sleepy from his ordeal and found a chair with a padded cushion on it and fell asleep.

Later that day, Romeo woke up and saw that the door had been left open part way so he walked outside to rejoin his sister and mama.

Following the rescue, the man always brought dry cat food to the cats living in the barn twice a day. The food was a good quality and the cats' coats began to fill out and shine. The kittens grew into pretty cats. The little family thrived in the barn. They avoided the area around the well. They made friends with the horse, named "Beauty." Beauty was appropriately named. The horse was chestnut brown, lithe and healthy, with big expressive eyes. He was a calm horse, who rarely made a fuss. He placidly ate the hay provided and was glad when he was let out to run and exercise in the yard. He was careful not to step on the cats' tails and watched over them protectively.

Life was good for Romeo, Juliet, and Mama. The barn was cozy, they were well-fed, and there were no major predators in the vicinity. An occasional stray dog would run through the yard and the fields, but other than that, it was a good cat life for the little family. The man paid more attention to them and they adjusted well to an outdoor lifestyle, which was all they had ever known.

Life wasn't as kind to the man. As a farmer living on acres of farmland, he worked hard to make a decent living. He was used to the long hours and labor-intensive work, but he saw that many of his neighbors were selling their property to developers who would turn the rolling hills and wooded areas into subdivisions where many houses were built. Soon, development was encroaching upon him. No longer could he look out from his back yard and see hills and valleys and trees for miles. Instead, what he saw made him very sad. The vast green spaces were now built up with small home sites. Houses were now cluttering the landscape. The houses were laid out in neat and tidy rows, but there wasn't much variation in them. One could come home and get lost trying to find the right house. The large trees had been removed for the benefit of the bulldozers and developers and small, spindly ones had been planted that would take many years to grow tall. The whine of chainsaws was constant, while they sawed up the old large oaks and elms and poplars that had graced the area. Traffic had increased on the back roads in his neighborhood. The roads were being paved, which enabled the cars to speed faster and more recklessly. He had to be careful when he crossed the road to pick up his mail so that he didn't get hit by a speeding car or truck. There was even a stoplight installed about a half mile down the road where there had formerly been a dirt crossroads.

The man's land had been in his family for generations, with his ancestors making their living as farmers as he had for years. An old log cabin was still standing at the corner of the back yard, which the man maintained meticulously. His great-grandmother had been born in the cabin and it had become a treasured relic over the years. The man loved the cabin and sometimes spent hours on its small front porch in a rocking chair reading and enjoying the feeling of connection to his past.

He continued to tend the crops in the fields and take care of his cows. But he could see the writing on the wall. He had been approached several times by various developers wanting to buy his property for a tidy sum, but he had declined each time. But now, as he was growing older, he knew that he couldn't keep up the pace that he had set for himself years ago. He began to think that a smaller place would be right for him in his old age. Maybe a place where someone could cook for him and tidy up a bit. Many of his long-time neighbors were already gone. He didn't blame them for selling out because he knew that they could use the money. He loved his lifestyle, his farm, and the fresh country air but he knew he wouldn't be able to continue in his present state for much longer.

The turning point came sooner than he had expected. One day a man called him and asked if he could pay a visit. When the man knocked on the farmer's door, he was dressed in a navy blue suit and was wearing a red tie. The farmer thought this didn't bode well for him. The suit man discussed the farmer's property as if a decision had already been made. The gist of the conversation was that the property was eventually going to be turned into a highway to help with the overflow of new traffic in the neighborhood, even without the farmer's consent. Something about "eminent domain" and "fair market value." The farmer kept mostly quiet. He asked a few questions but he already knew the answers.

When the man had finished his speech, he left and the farmer went out to sit on the porch of his log cabin. He sat there for a long time thinking. The cats emerged from the barn and went over to him and rubbed against his ankles. He reached down to pet them and scratch their heads. One by one, they found a spot on the porch and lay down to take a nap in the sunshine. The farmer also nodded off for a while. The surrounding area was unusually quiet without the whine of the chainsaws and without the sound of heavy trucks making their way down the once empty roads. The farmer dreamed about an earlier time, when the countryside was peaceful and calm. This was his home, the only home he had ever known, except for the time he spent in the Army. He began dreaming that there were guns shooting and the sound hurt his ears. He wanted the noise to stop so he could continue his pleasant dream, but the loud noise continued. Finally he awoke and realized it was not gunshots, but more construction noise from some distance away. He gazed at his cats napping lazily on the porch and wondered what would happen to them once he had left. He knew they couldn't go with him, but he couldn't leave them to fend for themselves. This was a dilemma he would have to resolve.

He then began thinking about the cabin. The old cabin was in good shape and had held up well over the years. He couldn't leave it here to be torn down like so many of the old trees. An idea occurred to him. There was an historical museum in the neighboring county that showcased how life had been generations ago. Re-enactors dressed up in period costume and showed visitors around the grounds. There was a blacksmith and a cooper who made real barrels. Other people played the part of carpenters, teachers, and preachers. The museum drew visitors from everywhere and the farmer had visited it several times over the years. He decided that he would inquire if the museum would like to have the old cabin if he donated it to them. They would have to disassemble it and number each piece and then reassemble it on the museum grounds. Yes, he thought he would call them tomorrow. He tried to resume his nap as the sun moved across the sky and left long shadows on the porch.

The cats knew something was different that day. Two trucks pulled up and men began removing equipment and carrying it to the old cabin. The cats hid in the barn but were able to peek out from a window to watch the action. The farmer came out and sat in his chair for the last time and stared at the green hills. Soon, he felt like he was in the way so he moved his chair onto the lawn so he could keep tabs on the work that was beginning. He hoped that his great-grandmother would approve of his choice and he felt like she would, considering the circumstances.

Day after day, the trucks came and slowly the cabin vanished. Where it once stood, proud and sturdy, the old rock foundation was now exposed. The rocks seemed to cry out, "Where is the old place where so much of life had happened over so many years?" But only silence answered them. The timelessness of the earth could have swallowed them.

Romeo and Juliet and Mama were nervous. Changes were coming and cats don't like change. The farmer seemed to be paying more attention to them lately, more than he had ever done. He wasn't working his fields like he usually did. One day, a large trailer pulled up and began loading the cows into it. The cows were separated from their calves and the calves protested loudly. Bawling calves made the cats even more agitated.

Soon, the cows were gone, too. The cats had watched as they were driven off, to who knows where. Beauty, the horse, was confined to his stall. When the farmer walked down to the barn one morning, he was carrying a cat cage. He opened the barn door and called the cats' names. Obediently, all three cats came to him, expecting some food or petting. The farmer picked up Juliet and Mama and placed them gently in the cage.

The farmer kept saying, "I'm sorry. I'm so sorry."

Romeo was wondering what was happening. As he saw them being carried out, he became frantic. He ran after the farmer and tried to step in front of his feet as the farmer kept walking toward his truck.

"Where are you going?" Romeo cried. Of course, the farmer didn't know what he was saying, but he could sense the feeling of despair in Romeo's voice.

"My mama and sister! Where are you taking them?"

"Juliet! Mama!"

Juliet and Mama meowed in perplexity. They had never been caged, much less experienced the feeling of being put into the cab of a truck. They took one last, long look at Romeo and cried. Romeo whimpered pitifully. He was losing his family, the only family he had ever had.

"I'm so sorry. They have to go live with my daughter and her children. She only wanted the females," the farmer told Romeo as if he knew he would understand his words. Romeo was stunned. He crouched down in the grass, bewildered and confused. As the farmer started the truck and drove away, Romeo could still hear his sister's and mama's plaintive cries echo in his head. They were gone. Romeo was alone. He walked slowly and dejectedly back to the barn, not even stopping to pay attention to the little white butterfly flitting across the path. He went to the corner and curled up and hid his face underneath his tail.

Later, Beauty came in and nudged Romeo with his nose. Romeo tried to ignore the horse, but Beauty was insistent. Romeo reached out his paw to push the horse away, but Beauty looked deep into Romeo's eyes and conveyed his sympathy. They weren't able to verbally communicate, but they could understand each other in non-verbal ways. And so the horse and the cat spent a few days close to each other in the old barn. Romeo tried not to think about his mama and his sister. He tried to forget the time he had fallen down the well and they and the farmer had rescued him. He tried to forget the warmth of their bodies on the cold winter nights. He snuggled up to the horse and slept as much as he could.

Soon after Juliet and Mama had been taken away, the farmer came down the pathway again carrying the cage. Romeo didn't care. If he was to live somewhere else and with someone else, he was indifferent. He didn't have a chance to say goodbye to Beauty because the horse was out in the field. The farmer put Romeo into the cage and then into the truck. They drove to the shelter in silence and after the farmer had left Romeo at the shelter, he trudged back to his truck, put his head on the steering wheel, and finally, he cried.

A RESCUE

The man in the flannel shirt lay still on the ground. What had happened to him? Did he have a heart attack? What could I do to help him? I was just a cat. Slowly I crept closer to him and saw that his eyes were closed. I could detect small breaths and his chest was moving slightly. Maybe he had hit his head and was unconscious. I tiptoed a little closer. He was a very large man and his size somewhat frightened me, but since he wasn't moving, I was more curious than scared. Edging my way almost to his feet, I smelled his body. It wasn't unpleasant; it was a manly smell with a hint of cut wood. I sniffed his shoes and they gave off an aroma of a mixture of cow manure and mud. Slowly and carefully I moved up to his face. He had dark hair, cropped short and a suggestion of a very short graying beard. His cap had fallen off his head and was lying in the dirt. I could smell his breath now and I put out my paw and touched his forehead. It was smooth to my touch. I knew that licking a wound will help to heal it, so I thought that maybe if I licked his face, he would revive. I began to lick his forehead and then moved down to his cheeks. My rough tongue tasted his perspiration and the salt was not unpleasant. I continued to lick his face.

All of a sudden, the man's eyes opened and he stared directly into my eyes. That startled me so I backed away slowly, always keeping my eyes on his. He watched me move away and then I heard him groan painfully. His right hand reached out toward me, and I continued to back away.

"Come here," he whispered.

I didn't want to go any closer so I just sat and looked at him.

"Help me," he exhaled.

What did he expect me to do? I could sense that he wouldn't hurt me, so I put one foot in front of the other and went to him. He had again closed his eyes and I tapped gently on his face. He didn't respond so I decided to use my purring abilities to try to save him. Purring is very therapeutic for both humans and cats so I sat on his chest and began to purr. I purred loudly and constantly. I kneaded his chest slowly and purred some more. I flexed and retracted my claws so as not to hurt him. My purrs rumbled through my body and I transmitted them to his body. After some time, I could tell his breathing was becoming more regular and was deeper. The man reached out and touched me. I didn't mind this. He stroked my back a few times.

"Kitty cat, I think you've just saved my life."

How did he know my name? I continued my therapy as he tried to shift a bit from his position. Another moan escaped his lips and he put his hand on his head. I could tell it was painful to touch. He then tried to sit up, but the effort was too much for him so he just lay back down on the ground. I made myself comfortable on his chest. We rested that way for quite a while.

Finally, he aroused and dragged himself over to his truck and opened the door. He reached in and found his cell phone on the seat. I watched him as he moved unsteadily. He began talking on his phone and I could detect the sound of a woman's voice on the other end. He told her what had happened and where he was. She must have told him to stay there and that she would be right over. I knew this was time to make my exit, but I wanted to watch him until the woman came.

"What can I do for you? You must be a stray because you're not very skittish. You helped me and stayed by my side while I was out. Are you hungry?" He touched the number on his phone, but there was no answer.

"Oh, I should have told her to bring some cat food for you," he said to me. "Wait! I have some Vienna sausages here in the glove compartment. Maybe you'd like them."

He reached in the truck and fumbled around in the glove compartment until he found the little can. Popping the top, he took them out and found a leaf to put them on.

"Come on, they're for you."

I looked warily at him. It had been so long since I had eaten food offered by a human, I was unsure of the protocol. The sausages sure smelled good to me and I was hungry, as usual. I sauntered closer to the sausages and then reached out and grabbed one with my claws. Chomping down on it, I savored the taste. Mmmm, good! I ate the rest greedily and kept my eye on the man. He was sitting in his truck watching me.

"Where do you live, Kitty cat? Do you belong to someone?"

Noooo, I didn't belong to anyone. Cats don't belong to people; they merely coexist with them, unless they were like me, living on my own, a cat gone astray some time ago. I began to wash my paws and then my whiskers and my face. The lingering smell of the sausages was nice.

Presently I heard the sound of a car moving across the field toward us. I knew it was the woman, coming to see about the man. I looked at him one last time and moved into the shadow of the woods, where I could blend in with the fall leaves.

ROMEO IS ADOPTED

At the shelter, I fell into a routine. Sleep at night, breakfast, a morning nap, time in the playroom on some days, more naptime, dinner, and a bit of conversation with Ivory. Visitors came and went, checking out the cats. One day, I saw a middle-aged lady come in the adoption room. She was wearing jeans and a stylish sweater. As she walked slowly around the room, looking in the cages, she spoke softly to the cats that were awake. She left the sleeping cats alone. A few cats spoke to her and she talked to them in a soothing voice. As she approached Romeo's cage, he reached out to her and she took his paw. He turned sideways and rubbed against the bars of the cage. The lady asked the attendant if she could take Romeo out of the cage. Romeo was picked up and put in the lady's arms. He immediately put his arms around her neck and nuzzled her. Wow! It looked like a perfect match! The lady put Romeo on the floor and he wrapped himself around her ankles. He marked her jeans with his whisker pads and stepped on her feet. He knew what to do. I was taking notes on his behavior. They really seemed to bond right away. The attendant was watching the interaction and commented on the way Romeo and the lady looked like they belonged together. The lady said yes, she thought so, too.

"I want this one," she stated.

Romeo was being adopted! I was so glad for him and sad for myself because I was losing my friend. The attendant took the lady's cage that she had brought and put Romeo into it. She picked up a bag of cat food that is given to all adopters and Romeo looked over at me and Ivory and said goodbye.

"I hate to leave you guys, but this is my big chance. This lady is a real cat person and she wants me. I hope things work out," he told us.

"I hope you have a wonderful life, Romeo! Take care and be happy!"

"Goodbye!"

"Goodbye, Romeo," said some of the other cats.

Then they were gone. They made their way out to the reception room to fill out the paperwork. I was happy for him; he deserved a good life.

Ivory and I looked at each other.

"That's wonderful that he was adopted," said Ivory.

"Yeah, I'm glad for him."

"You know, one day it will also happen to us," she told me.

"I hope we can be adopted together."

"That probably won't happen. Most people only want one cat, not two."

"What would I do without you?" I asked her.

"You would hopefully lead a gentle and peaceful life in the company of a caring person or family. You can't count on me being there."

"Oh, it's too painful to think about," I said.

I retired to the back of my cage to try to forget about what we had discussed. I wanted to go to a good home and have a relationship with someone who would care for me, but I didn't want to leave Ivory. I had become attached to her and I almost felt like she was a part of me. She was right; the chances of us being together were slim. My future was up in the air and there was nothing I could do about it. All shelter animals faced the same situation. Some adapt more easily than others; some probably never do adapt to strange environments. One could only hope for a lucky break.

THE HAIRLESS CAT, SCORPIO

A few days later, one of the workers moved a cage beside mine. A cat was in it and I saw that it was the hairless one I had seen earlier. I read the tag on the outside of the cage and it said, "Scorpio." This was indeed a strange-looking cat. He had no fur at all, only baggy skin. He was a pretty gray color, but I wondered if he wasn't cold all the time. He had a narrow face and a pointed muzzle and very large ears. He looked like a little old man with very wrinkled skin. His eyes were big and expressive and I guess he could be considered pretty, in a different sort of way. He had the longest tail I had ever seen.

I decided to speak first. "Scorpio? Is that your name?"

"Yes, that's me."

"Did someone name you who was interested in astrology?"

"I guess they did. At least they didn't name me Sagittarius, Cancer or Capricorn."

I chuckled a bit at that.

"And you are…?"

"Kitty."

"Well, that's original."

"I'm hoping my new human will give me another name," I said.

"People name cats the weirdest names. They don't realize that the poor cat may be stuck with the name for his or her entire life. I once knew a cat named Bathsheba. They called her Sheba for short. The name one chooses says as much about the person as it does the cat. Then there was Astroturf, who must have been named by a football fan."

"Yeah, people should think about the cat's characteristics before pinning just any name on him or her," I stated.

"How long have you been here?" he asked.

"Oh, for weeks. I've lost track of the time."

"I've been here for a couple of months now. I probably look funny to most people and that's why they pass me by. I'm just a normal cat, only without the fur."

"Do you get cold?"

"I get colder than other cats, but at least I've been indoors for most of my life, sheltered from the weather."

"What type of cat are you?"

"I'm a Sphynx. What type are you?" he inquired.

I paused. I didn't know what type I was.

"I guess I'm just a regular cat."

"You are a domestic longhair and also a calico," he stated after taking a good look at me. "Calicos are almost always females and in Japan they are considered lucky. If you had more stripes, you'd be considered a tabico."

That was a new one for me. This cat was full of information and had purrsonality plus.

"A tabico is a cross between a tabby and a calico."

Ivory spoke up, "I'm white, but if you look closely, I have tabby markings."

Scorpio said, "That's right. Even black cats can be tabbies."

I was getting quite an education. I asked, "Where did you come from?"

He answered, "Well, I had a great life with my human companions. They purchased me from a breeder when I was little."

I interrupted, "They paid money for you?" This was incomprehensible to me. I thought to myself, why pay for cats when there were so many homeless ones who were free, or low-cost at the shelter?

"Oh yes, quite a bit of money. My people had money and we lived in a big house. There was also a housekeeper, a gardener, and a cook who lived there. I never wanted for anything. Even though my people were gone most of the time, traveling or working at their jobs, I had plenty of company from the paid people who were full-time. I was well-fed and well-taken care of. I lived like a king!"

I was trying to absorb what Scorpio was saying. Ivory was listening quietly in her cage, too. We understood that Scorpio had lived a much different life than we had.

"So what happened?" I asked.

"Well, one day my people came home and they had a very quiet conversation with the housekeeper, cook, and gardener. I tried to listen, but their voices were hushed and I couldn't hear everything they were saying. But I did pick up the phrases, "moving to Italy" and "selling the house." That's when my whole world began to collapse. Preparations were made to put the house on the market. Real estate agents appeared and a contract was signed. The gardener started sprucing up the grounds and the house was made to sparkle and shine. Everything always had to be in its place in case a prospective buyer wanted to see the house. I wasn't getting as much attention as I was used to. I kept wondering what was going to happen to me and if I should start brushing up on my Italian. But the plans didn't include me. My people said they couldn't take me to Italy and they didn't know what to do with me. I felt lost, even though I still lived in the house."

"The movers came and began to pack up all the belongings, the antique furniture, and everything else. I tried to stay out of the way and hid in an upstairs bedroom, but soon, they came into the room and began to move the furniture out. I ran out and went down into the kitchen. The kitchen was bare! The table and chairs were gone and all the appliances were packed into big cardboard boxes. I felt so alone. Everything that was familiar to me was either gone or packed."

"Then I saw it. The cage was brought out and the housekeeper put me into it. I didn't even have a chance to say goodbye to my people. And that's how I ended up here, in a shelter with all the other throw-aways." He began to weep.

"It's okay, Scorpio. It's okay," I tried to reassure him. "Don't feel bad. At least you had a chance to live like a king. Most of us have had a much harder life."

"No one will want me because I don't have any fur. I'm not soft and cuddly like most cats."

I told him, "But you are unusual. You are unique. People like cats that are different and not like every day, run of the mill."

Scorpio continued to sob.

Ivory whispered, "Leave him alone. He'll settle down after a while." So I tucked my paws underneath me and closed my eyes. I sighed. Everyone had a different story here at the shelter.

HISSED OFF: SPUNKY

The next interesting cat I discovered was Spunky. Spunky wasn't a likeable cat. He was just the opposite. He would lash out at everyone who tried to even look at him. His claws were wicked, too. I think the vet tech was afraid of him and didn't want to trim his claws, so they remained like little razors, ready to slash. Spunky was black, all black. His fur was thick and glossy. His green eyes were a beautiful contrast to his fur. Black cats have less of a chance of being adopted than other cats. He would probably be at the shelter for a while. He not only had an attitude, he had a cattitude, which was infinitely worse.

Someone at the shelter had named him since he probably didn't even have a name when he arrived. That someone was hoping he would mellow but still live up to the name. "Spunky" was an understatement. The name brought to mind similar words, like "lively" and "energetic". He was all that and more with an added dash of meanness.

Spunky had lived a number of years as a feral, fending for himself on the streets of a city. He was streetwise and tough. He also sported a few battle scars that included a notched ear, a permanent scratch across his nose, and a shortened tail. No one knew how his tail was cut off and the other cats were afraid to ask him.

He arrived at the shelter after being trapped in a humane trap. It was probably from a roundup of several stray and feral cats that were being bothersome by foraging in trash cans and hanging out in alleyways. These poor cats were just trying to survive and stay alive. Some had been thrown out, others had been born feral. Survival on the streets is risky and dangerous and cats had to develop a sixth and seventh sense about how to navigate the perils that awaited them every day. The day he was trapped, he went wild. He almost tore up the metal bars of the cage trying to escape. He had avoided traps like this one for years, but this time he let down his guard because he was hungry. Hunger was a permanent state with Spunky and the other city cats. The trap had been baited with canned cat food and he just couldn't resist the smell. He knew the trap was something to avoid, but he tried it anyway. Stepping inside, he made his way cautiously to the back of the trap. When his foot hit the metal plate, the door slammed shut behind him and he was caught. He freaked out. The dish of cat food went flying, spilling food everywhere. He banged around inside, screeching and yelling. Hurting himself in his tirade, he didn't care. He just wanted out.

Soon, a man came by and threw a blanket over the trap so Spunky couldn't see anything. This was meant to calm him down, but Spunky didn't want to calm down. He continued to fling himself violently against the bars. The man then picked up the cage with the blanket concealing the cage and put it in the back of a truck. Spunky continued to howl. The driver of the truck took Spunky to the shelter.

When they entered the door, Spunky knew that this was bad news. He was no longer free. He was caged and couldn't get out. His nose was bleeding and his paws were hurt from where he had attacked the sides of the cage, trying to escape. He crouched at the back of the cage and waited. The person on duty wouldn't reach in to move him to another cage so he had to spend several days in the trap, eating very little and using a small litter box, which he loathed. He was very angry, not only at the man who trapped him, but at himself for letting down his guard. Whenever someone put food in the cage or tried to remove the litter box for cleaning, he would try to slash their hands. He would growl menacingly and hiss and spit in their direction. He was getting a bad reputation as an incorrigible. His anger was constant and he used up a lot of energy being angry. His eyes flashed when someone walked past the cage. His body became cramped from staying in one position for hours on end. He stopped grooming himself and his beautiful black coat started looking unkempt and ratty.

One day when his food was brought out, he could smell something different in the food. He waited until the worker had left and sniffed it carefully. He didn't know what was wrong, but he decided to eat it anyway. After a while he started to become sleepy. This wasn't his usual nap time and it dawned on him that the food must have been drugged. He was falling asleep and he tried his best to stay awake, but he couldn't help dozing off.

Spunky awoke in a different cage and in a different part of the building. There was a soft, fluffy blanket underneath him. He smelled himself and didn't like what he detected. His fur had the smell of humans and he hated humans. Humans had been handling him! He examined his claws and found that someone had trimmed his claws. They were no longer the razor sharp defenders he had always relied on. His back hip also stung where they must have given him a shot. He began to lick himself all over to rid himself of the human scent. He was groggy and felt bad. He did notice that this cage had more room than the trap had. He was at least able to move around a bit, but he felt awful and just wanted to be out of the cage. He despised the cage. He despised the people and the shelter and everything that his life had degenerated into.

It was then that he saw his testicles were gone! Gone! Where were they? He looked closer and discovered that they were actually still there, but had shrunk. He must have been neutered! His manhood had been taken away while he had been drugged. No more carousing with females and no more becoming a "father" who didn't pay attention to his own kittens. He was ruined as a stud tom cat. At least that's what he had thought of himself.

I met Spunky some time later in the playroom. The attendants had moved his cage into the room, but wouldn't let him out for fear that they would never be able to coax him back into it. I was playing on the cat tree, climbing up and down and flexing my claws on the wrapped trunk when he was brought in. The cage was put in a corner so Spunky could look out at the other cats having fun and interacting with one another. I guess the theory was that if he could see normal behavior in other cats, he may want to emulate them. He had a sullen look on his face and if a cat moved too close to his cage, he growled. Soon, the others began to ignore him and go about their business, playing with the toys.

I felt sorry for him, but I was also afraid of him. I knew he couldn't hurt me since he was in the cage so I walked slowly up to him. He looked at me with those terrible eyes and let out a menacing growl. I just watched him from a few feet away. He began to hiss and I sat down in front of his cage. He snarled at me again and bared his fangs. His fur began to stand on end and his spine became a razorback.

"Why the attitude?" I asked him.

"Grrrrr!" he replied.

"I'm just a kitten; I can't hurt you."

"Ssssstt!" he scowled.

"Haven't you ever heard the expression, 'Purr more, hiss less'?" I inquired.

No answer was forthcoming.

"It's not so bad, is it?"

"I hate you," he said through a clenched jaw, showing his pointed teeth.

"Why? I haven't done anything to you."

"I hate all cats, especially little ones like you," he growled.

"Well, I can't help being little. I just thought you might want to be friends."

"Friends? Ha! I don't have any friends and I don't want any."

"Friends are good for you. They improve your attitude and help you."

"My attitude doesn't need improving."

"Oh, well, that explains it."

"Explains what?" he wanted to know.

"Your attitude. If you acted more friendly, things wouldn't be so hard for you. Besides, being in a bad mood all the time is not good for your health."

"What do you care about my health?" he asked.

"Don't you want to live to a ripe old age?"

"No, I don't. I just want out of here."

"If you were friendly, you'd have a better chance of getting out of here. People don't want a cat that acts like you do. If you continue to act like a jerk, you'll spend the rest of your life in a cage."

"I hate people. I don't want to live with anyone. All I want is to go back to where I came from."

"Where did you come from?"

He began to tell me about his life on the busy streets and how he had to scrounge for food and how he starved and how he had to endure all types of weather and how he had to find safe places to sleep and how he had to fight other cats sometimes and avoid dogs and other animals. He had to keep away from speeding cars in the streets and keep away from mean people in the city. He had come to distrust everyone who he had contact with in his life.

"It sounds to me like it's better to be in the cage than on the street. Here, at least they feed you, they try to turn you into an adoptable cat, and if you let them, they would shower you with affection."

"I can't stand the thought of anyone touching me. The only contact I've ever had with people is when they drugged me and I wasn't aware of it."

"But how do you know you don't like it if you've never tried it?" I asked.

"Well, I just don't."

"Let one of the workers pet you and don't growl or snarl or hiss at him or her. See what happens."

"No, I don't want to touch them."

"Ok, how about if I let you touch my paw?" I asked him. "I won't hurt you."

Silence. I reached out my little paw and put it close to his cage. He looked at it for a while and then tentatively reached out and brushed the tips of my claws with his own. He then laid his paw over mine and left it there. A few of the other cats started whispering and looking in our direction.

"Look, Spunky is touching Kitty."

"Wow. I hope she has health insurance."

"Maybe he'll be a bit more friendly to us now."

"No, he's a feral. He hates cats."

"Hey, Spunk, is she your girlfriend?" a big orange tomcat teased. Spunky narrowed his eyes.

I said, "Just ignore them. See, it's not so bad. I'll come a little closer and you can touch my forehead." So I went up to the cage and moved my head close to the bars. Spunky reached out and put his paw on top of my head. More of the cats began to stare at us.

"Boy, she's brave."

"He hasn't slashed her yet."

"She has such a pretty face, I'd hate to see him mangle it."

I told him, "Ok, that's probably enough for today. We'll try something else tomorrow."

He replied, "Ok, it wasn't as bad as I thought it would be."

"Maybe you can think about having one of the attendants touch you."

"I don't know. I'll consider it."

"Just let your anger go. Shrug off those negative feelings. Think positive thoughts about how nice a soft touch would be, and a gentle hand to caress your fur."

The next day in the playroom, Spunky did not growl or hiss or snarl at us. He just watched us warily as we romped with our toys. One of the human volunteers came around and gave each of us a treat which we gobbled up. The volunteer walked over to Spunky's cage and asked him if he'd like a treat. Spunky just looked up at her so she placed the treat inside the bars without opening the cage. She then sat down in a chair not far from Spunky's cage. He reached out and pulled the treat close to him and then ate it. The volunteer smiled and gave him another treat. He ate this one, also.

"I see you aren't quite so afraid of me anymore," she said to him. "Maybe one day, I'll be able to pet you."

Spunky grumbled under his breath. The volunteer laughed softly. I ambled close to the cage and rubbed against the bars. The volunteer reached out to stroke my back and head and I marked her with my whisker pads. She placed me on her lap and I kneaded her leg.

As she massaged my spine, I told Spunky, "Look, it feels good. Let her touch you."

"No."

A few days passed, and gradually, Spunky lost some of his fear of humans. The same volunteer came every day and gave him treats. One day, she opened the door to his cage. He looked out and saw that he would be able to escape. But even if he did, he would still be in the room with all the other cats, who he didn't like, so he remained in his cage. Eventually, curiosity got the better of him, however, and he poked his head out. The volunteer held out her hand with a treat in it, which Spunky sniffed. She then put it a few inches outside the cage and Spunky stepped out to eat it. The volunteer touched his head at the same time and he didn't pull away or lash out at her. Score one for the volunteer!

The volunteer spent more time with Spunky over the next few days and he became less wary and more outgoing. The lady started to pet him for a few seconds and then it became a few minutes. Gradually, Spunky let her scratch him under the chin and massage his neck. He loosened up and even became a bit more friendly toward some of the other cats. He no longer growled when a cat came near him. His hisses became less frequent. Soon, he was allowed out of his cage during playtime. At first he stayed near his cage, but then he began to wander around the room and marveled at all the cat toys available to him. He picked up a catnip mouse and threw it up in the air and carried it across the room. He batted it around for a while and then discovered a crinkly toy that made a noise when he touched it. A box that looked like a piece of cardboard cheese drew his interest and when he put his paw into one of the holes, a mouse popped up from another hole. What joy! What cat heaven!

He also spent quite a bit of time with me. He would groom me and lick the back of my neck where my tongue couldn't reach. I would do the same for him. He became my friend and I was happy that I had been able to draw him out of his shell. It was almost like he was a different cat. He actually seemed to enjoy living at the shelter and was becoming what they would call "adoptable." His black fur gleamed in the sunlight and his eyes shone like bright green marbles. He seemed to relish the contact from people and a few other cats. His attitude changed and he looked forward to playtime and to other activities at the shelter.

The volunteer decided to take Spunky home with her to socialize him even more. She had two older children who loved cats and a dog that got along well with cats. On the day Spunky was to leave, we all said our goodbyes. It was a tearful time for me because I had been his first friend. I knew he would be well taken care of, but I also knew I probably wouldn't see him again.

He came over to my cage and said, "If it hadn't been for you, I would have been lost. You helped me in so many ways, I can never thank you enough. You took an interest in me where others just dismissed me as a wild and feral cat. Your tender touch opened up a whole new world for me and now I may even have a home for good."

"No cat is too wild to have friends. Everyone needs friends and everyone needs to be touched. I just happened to be there at the right time. Everyone gets second chances and you've been given yours. Take care, Spunky. Hope you have a good life."

"Goodbye, Kitty. I hope the right person adopts you soon, too," he said.

And Spunky was gone.

MONIQUE

More cats were brought into the adoption room. The cages were crammed together and we felt like packed sardines in a can. I noticed again that some of the kittens were adopted faster than the older cats. Not many black cats were adopted. That was a shame because black cats make great pets, just like any of the rest of us. Some people are superstitious and think they are bad luck. I did find out that the shelter didn't allow any black cats to be adopted during the month of October because they were afraid the cats would be used for ill purposes on Halloween. That was a good policy.

I was semi-napping one afternoon when I saw a nicely-dressed woman come in the adoption room. She wore fashionable clothes that complimented her overall demeanor. Her black hair was professionally done and her nails were manicured perfectly. She moved with grace and assurance, like a cat. Her dark eyes scanned the room and took in the multitude of cages and the cats who inhabited them. As I opened my eyes to check her out, she looked over at me and smiled. I stood up and stretched and rubbed my cheeks against the bars. The lady walked over to my cage and put out her hand. I sniffed it and she put her finger in my cage. I admired the nail polish and looked up at her. I am always aware of nails since I groom mine constantly and try to keep them in top condition.

She summoned the volunteer in the room and indicated she would like to take a closer look at me. My cage door was opened and I fluffed my tail a little bit. She reached in and picked me up. Holding me up, she turned me around and inspected my coat, petting my back and speaking in a soothing voice.

"You look very sweet. What's your name?" she asked. She then looked up at the sign on my cage that said, "KITTY" and laughed.

"Kitty? Who gave you that name?"

I began to knead her arm. Ivory woke up and came to the front of her cage to see what was going on.

"You're a pretty white cat, too," she told Ivory. Ivory reached out a paw and the lady took it. She put me on the floor and I started to wrap myself around her ankles, just as I had seen Romeo do. She seemed to like this, so I reached up and gently put my paws on her knee, keeping my claws carefully sheathed.

"Oh, you're so cute! I think you like me."

Ivory kept watching my performance. "Meow at her," Ivory told me.

I gave a little squeak of a meow and acted cute.

The lady asked the volunteer, "How long has she been here?"

"Well, quite a while. You can see how many cats are up for adoption and more keep coming in every day."

"She has a lovely coat and coloring."

"Yes, she's a pretty calico. She gets along with the other cats and she likes people," the volunteer encouraged.

"I wonder if she would get along with a dog?"

Uh oh. A dog! So far all my experiences with dogs had been negative. I had been hoping that I wouldn't have to deal with any more dogs.

"Well, I don't know. If you have a dog at home, you could try her and if there is a conflict, you could always bring her back."

My heart began to sink. I didn't want to live with another dog. Dogs were rowdy and noisy and bothersome.

"Well, I really like her and she's so attractive."

Then a thought crossed my mind. If she adopted me, I'd be leaving Ivory. I'd probably never see Ivory again! My tail drooped and I looked up at Ivory. She was smiling at me.

"You have to take a chance. If this is the right person, you have to give her the benefit of the doubt. She acts like she's a cat person even if she has a dog. And who knows, you might even like the dog. Not all of them are the same."

"But I'd be leaving you! I want you to come with me! You're my best friend!" I cried.

The lady said, "I'd like to take Kitty home with me." She picked me up and I reached out and grabbed the bars of Ivory's cage and wouldn't let go. I was clinging to it and the nice lady was trying to make me loosen my grip.

Ivory put her face close to mine and kissed me. She said, "Maybe we'll meet again when we go over the Rainbow Bridge."

I cried. I held on as tightly as I could, but then Ivory said, "Go ahead. Remember I love you."

"I don't think she wants to leave the white cat," the lady told the volunteer.

"Yeah, they've been close to each other ever since Kitty arrived here."

My body shuddered and I released the bars. I was put into a carrying cage and I kept my eyes on Ivory. She watched me and our eyes met for the last time as I was carried out of the adoption room.

At the desk, the lady filled out the paperwork. The clerk asked her name and she said, "Monique Jackson." So, I was going to be living with Monique from now on.

I crunched down in the cage, still so upset at leaving Ivory and closed my eyes. There was nothing I could do about it. Again, I had no control over what was happening to me. People always seemed to be running my life, making me do things and choosing the direction of my life path which was a crooked and winding one.

I overheard the clerk saying, "If you think money can't buy happiness, you've never paid to adopt a cat." I agreed with her, even though I was feeling so dejected. When the paperwork was completed and the fee paid, we left the shelter. I was put in the front seat of a car and we began our new life together by driving away from the shelter and away from Ivory.

I didn't make any noise while we were heading toward my new home. Monique talked to me sometimes and sometimes she sang along with the songs on the radio. She switched the channel to a classical music station and the melodies soothed me a little bit. Piano music by Chopin was good for my poor cat soul. Sadly I thought about Ivory and the conversations we had. She was such a sweet and gentle cat, maybe someone good would adopt her soon. I hoped she would have a happy life even though I would miss her terribly. I'd probably never have another friend like Ivory and my little heart was heavy.

After a while, we pulled in to a garden-style apartment building parking lot. I looked through the cage up at the building and could see the bricks and windows. Monique parked the car and came around to get my cage. Carrying me was easy for her because I didn't weigh much and she seemed to be in good physical shape.

I was carried up a short flight of stairs and when Monique opened the door I knew I was in trouble. There was an overwhelming odor of dog emanating from the apartment. Not being used to it, I covered my nose with my paw and retreated to the back of the cage. As I peered out I saw a well-appointed room with typical furniture and a large bay window where rays of sunshine poured through. Monique put the cage in the middle of the floor and opened the door. I stayed put.

"Come on, it's all right. This is your new home." I had heard those words before. She got down on the floor beside the cage and put her hand in. She smelled like a delicate spring wind which was not unpleasant.

I didn't see a dog, so reluctantly I took a tentative step outside the cage. Monique stroked my neck and back to reassure me. She had a light touch on my fur.

"Are you afraid of dogs?" she asked. "Buster won't hurt you. He won't hurt a fly. He's used to living with cats." Well, that was good news. Maybe he wasn't a typical dog.

"You'll like him once you guys become friends." I took another step out of the cage and sniffed the air. I wondered where was this friendly dog. The carpet felt good under my paws and I stretched to relieve some of the tension of the last few hours. I let Monique scratch me under the chin. I took a longer look around the room and spotted a couch and chair where I could take refuge if I needed to.

"You can explore all you want. Are you hungry? Let's see what I have in the kitchen for you." She started to walk into another room which I assumed was the kitchen so I followed her. Ah! Counters where I could jump on once I became a little bigger. Cat and counters really go well together. Especially kitchen counters where food was prepared. But right now, I was still too small to jump all the way up there.

I continued to look around for Buster, the dog, but didn't see him. My olfactory senses were still attuned to the dog smell, but I was becoming used to it. Monique opened a can and I immediately smelled the cat food, which she put into a dish and put on the floor. I started to eat, but suddenly I heard a noise behind me. I swirled around and there stood a big, shaggy black dog in the doorway. Buster had obviously smelled the cat food, too.

"Stay, Buster," Monique commanded him.

Buster didn't make a move to come into the kitchen, but just stood there looking at me and began to wag his tail. That was a good sign, but I was still wary of this black behemoth. Buster swayed a bit as he stood watching me. He was much taller than I was and probably weighed a good 70 pounds. I looked around for a place to escape, but all I could see was a kitchen table and some chairs. The chairs would have to do if need be. I wouldn't be out of his reach, but at least I would be looking down on him, somewhat.

Buster seemed to be a well-behaved dog, allowing me to eat without making a move toward me or the food dish. I nibbled a bit more and watched him out of the corner of my eye. He sort of slumped down and put his head on his paws. I had encountered such badly-behaved dogs in my short life that this one puzzled me. He actually listened to Monique. I began to relax and my muscles were less tense than they had been. This dog was old, almost ancient. As I looked in his eyes, I could see the cloudiness, the cataracts. The dark eyes were animated and he lifted his eyebrows at me. He didn't seem disturbed by my presence at all. He was gray around the muzzle and when he moved slightly it seemed to pain him. He had thick black fur, but it looked well-groomed without mats or clumps that so often accompanied old age.

I finished the food and washed my face. I even felt a bit secure, which was a new feeling for me, especially being in such close quarters with an unfamiliar dog. Buster watched me with a look of interest on his face. I decided to make a bold move and walked slowly over to him. He perked up a bit and I touched my nose to his. His tail began to move like a black plume waving in the breeze. He stretched out a paw and I sniffed it.

Buster wagged his tail and acknowledged my overture. I wondered whether he knew how to speak in cat language since Monique said he had lived with cats before. Maybe we could even be friends.

"Meow?" I asked him.

"Yeah, I can speak a bit of the cat language. I'm Buster as you probably already know. What's your name?" he questioned.

"I'm Kitty."

"Well, that's not very original...not to offend you."

"Oh, it doesn't offend me. I don't particularly like that name, but that's what I've been called." I was curious about him. "How old are you?"

"I'm about 14 or 15. How old are you?"

"Well, I'm not yet a year old, but sometimes I feel like I'm older."

"Why do you feel older?"

"I've been through a lot in my life." I began to tell him about my first home and the terrible time I had there. I told him about Beau, the puppy and what had happened to me when I went outside. I continued to talk about how I was taken to the shelter and my experiences there. When I started talking about Ivory, I felt sad because I knew I'd never see her again. Ivory had been such a good friend to me in those uncertain times at the shelter. Buster listened patiently as I described what had happened and how Monique chose me to come live with them.

"You'll like it here. Monique loves animals." Animals? I was a cat, not an animal. There's a difference. Cats are unique, not like other four legged creatures. Cats have one of the highest average IQs among non-human mammals. The region of the brain that deals with emotions is identical in humans and cats. Did Buster consider himself an "animal"?

"How long have you lived with Monique?" I asked him.

"Many, many years. I moved in with her when she finished high school and moved out of her mother's house. I've had a good life and now that I'm at the end of it, I don't have any regrets. She and I have been very close ever since she was young."

"So, there were other cats who lived with both of you?"

"Yes, there were three of them over the years. When Monique still lived with her mama, we all lived out in the country. There was Sam, an all-black cat who showed up from the woods one day, skinny as a rail. He had bite marks and scars over his entire body. Monique took him in and he turned into a very loving and sweet cat. All it took was some patience and he came around in no time. Soon his coat was shiny and he filled out to become sleek and beautiful." Buster moved slowly and painfully turned around to regard me.

"Then there was Sherlock. He was another woods cat and had been out on his own for years. Sherlock was a classic tabby with dark stripes, an "M" on his forehead, and a brindle coat. He also had a large head which happens in some unneutered male cats. He was wary at the beginning, but he was also hungry so he would sit in the front yard and wait until Monique came home from school to feed him. She has a way with animals (!) that makes them trust her." I didn't say anything to correct Buster about his use of the word "animal." No sense in offending him.

"The last cat was little Ginger. Ginger was a small cat, who weighed about 6 lbs. She never grew to be bigger, but always looked like a miniature feline. She, of course, was a ginger color with a white band around her back leg that looked like a bandage. I loved Ginger most of all. She was so gentle and kind to me. We'd sleep in the same bed and since her fur was very short, I provided some warmth when the weather turned cold. Gin was found in the middle of the road in front of our house. She came from a litter of kittens born under a house some distance away. She somehow made her way up the road and again, Monique took her in. She was tame and took to indoor living right away, but she still liked to slip outside every now and then to eat some grass and roll in the dirt. I miss her a lot." I didn't want to ask Buster what had happened to these cats. I just wanted to assume they had passed away from old age.

"So, they taught you to speak the cat language?" I asked him.

"Yes they did. Since there were no other dogs around, I wanted to be able to communicate with my cat companions. I don't know all the words, but I do know enough to be able to speak to you."

Monique returned from the other room. "It looks like you two are getting along just fine. Buster will show you around and make you comfortable, little one. Oh, I forget. . . I think we may change your name from Kitty to something else, something more appropriate. I'll watch you for a while to see what better name will suit you to fit your personality."

Yay! A name change! Just what I had been hoping for.

I wanted to explore the rest of the house. Buster told me that he'd take me around, but I told him I could manage it on my own. He seemed to have trouble getting up and down. He probably had arthritic knees and joints.

As I eased around the corner, I saw some very nice furniture that was upholstered in a nubby fabric! A nubby fabric! Just what cats love to sink their claws into. I instinctively knew that this may not be the correct thing to do right away, so I let that feeling pass. I did walk by and sniff the corners to see if there was any other cat aroma, but didn't detect any. Sam and Sherlock and Ginger must have been gone for a long time or else Monique had bought new furniture. I made sure to swipe my tail around a few of the corners just to let anyone know that I had been there recently.

I continued to explore the room. I saw a new scratching post in the corner and I ambled over to it. I could feel Monique watching me, so I stretched out my entire length and extended my claws into the sisal wrapped around the post.

"Oh, you're so smart! What an intelligent little cat!" she exclaimed. "You already know how to use the scratching post." Well, of course. All cats know what they are for; sometimes they just choose not to use them.

"What a clever kitty you are." Yes, I was. I arched my back like an upside down "U" and continued my walk. The dog smell didn't seem so pungent anymore and I guess I was getting used to it. It wasn't unpleasant; it was just a distinctive smell that only dogs could produce.

I peered into another room that was the bedroom. A large bed covered with a colorful quilt beckoned to me, so I jumped up on it. It smelled like Monique, clean and soft. I kneaded the quilt top and I could see Monique peeking around the corner, watching me.

"I have a little cat bed for you, next to where Buster sleeps, if you want to check it out," she told me. I thought I'd just sleep on the quilt, thank you. I wasn't very sleepy, but it was nap time and I turned around few times to make my nest. Time slipped away and I fell asleep and dreamed of my friend, Ivory.

MARIANA

The cats were hungry and Mariana was still asleep. The group was thinking the same thing: It's 7:00 a.m. and time to get up! Lily jumped up on the covers and began flexing her claws in the pillow next to Mariana's head. The others watched from the floor or stared out the window at a few early birds just awakening. Mariana's dark hair fanned out on the pillow as she snored lightly, trying to catch a few more ZZZs before it was time to start the day. The sun beamed through the window in shafts of yellow that highlighted the few wisps of free-floating dust. Charlie reached up to catch one, but it was elusive, disappearing beneath his paw. Cassidy stretched out full length on the carpet, lazily flicking her plume of a tail. Inbox was busy checking out the bluebird that was flying in and out of the nesting box located in front of the window.

Saturday mornings had always been a luxury for Mariana, allowing her extra time to sleep in without having to answer to an alarm clock. The habit remained, even after several years of retirement from her long-time job. Now there were the furry alarm clocks, awakening her each day demanding their breakfast. The alarm clocks were hungry! At least the sound of their voices was musically sweet to her ears, unlike the jangle of the clock. She had donated the electric clock to a worthy charity once the blessed day of retirement arrived. Her suits she had worn to work also wound up at the charity, hopefully to be adopted by some young up and coming working girl. Mariana hadn't worn a suit since.

Lily walked over Mariana's legs and tentatively touched her toes that were hidden beneath the covers. The toes moved a bit and Lily pounced, gently grabbing them with her paws. Mariana turned on her side and opened one sleepy eye and fixed Lily with a dazed expression.

"Surely you don't want breakfast already? You just ate dinner last night," Mariana told Lily. "My toes aren't for your breakfast." Lily again reached out to touch the other foot.

"Ohh, alright. You guys know how to keep a girl from getting any beauty sleep." Mariana rolled out of bed and the cats started swarming around her ankles, making it difficult for her to walk.

"If you want to eat, I have to be able to get to the kitchen," she told them. Inbox started batting at Cassidy and playing with her tail. Lily and Charlie began running toward the kitchen, which was the most important room in the house in their opinion.

The four cats had a very good life since they had moved in with Mariana. Each one had come to her separately and each had a story to tell about how he or she had found her. Lily was a rescue who Mariana had adopted from the shelter. She was a pretty cat with white paws and underside and gray on top. Her big eyes were enhanced with eyeliner and she had a sweet temperament. Lily was definitely a lap cat, seeking a warm lap even in the summertime. She had been with Mariana for about 7 years.

Charlie was a large orange and white cat with one eye. He originally had two eyes, like most cats did, but had developed problems and some years ago Mariana had the eye removed. He was able to function very well with only one eye and he looked rather debonair and rakish. Charlie was the oldest of the cats at around 14 years old and had slowed down somewhat in the past few years.

Cassidy had been a kitten when Mariana took her in. She was all black and had a petite build. With a mischievous look, and prone to getting in trouble, she sometimes tried Mariana's patience. At 4 years old, she still had a lot of kitten in her and could sometimes be found hiding under the covers, thinking, of course, that no one could see her. She loved to scratch her favorite chair, sharpening her claws and making her mark. Cassidy was a climber. Occasionally she could be seen hanging on the porch screen, stretching to catch a bug.

Inbox acquired his name because he loved to sleep in the box on the desk that held all the important papers that Mariana had to deal with every day. Inbox made it hard for her to work, sleeping and grooming in his favorite place. Inbox was a tuxedo cat, with classic black and white markings. He was a handsome cat and kept his coat in perfect condition. Inbox had a thing for Lily and the two got along well.

After breakfast, Mariana made her list of chores to do for the day. Bank, post office, grocery store, and a stop at the plant nursery. She was hoping that some plants would be on sale since it was now about mid-summer and the rush to spruce up yards and plant flowers had passed a few months before. She looked forward to getting out early the next day, and putting in some new flowers before the summer sun raised the temperature to miserable heights.

"Ok, guys, I'll be back in a while. I want everyone to behave and take naps while I'm gone," Mariana instructed the cats. The cats didn't need any prodding to engage in one of their favorite activities. Inbox retreated to his usual place, while the others stretched out in front of the window to catch some rays from the sun.

They were a contented group and Mariana was happy to be able to share her life with them.

As Mariana drove down the street, she began to think of her ex-husband, whom she had divorced many years ago. Thomas was still living in the area, working at a government job. They had married in their 20s, before they had a chance to really be on their own, supporting themselves individually. The marriage had started out well enough and continued for several years before Thomas decided that he didn't like being married. The real reason for the dissolution of the marriage was that he didn't like cats and Mariana was a cat person. She loved cats and always had. At that time, there were only three cats living with the couple, but Thomas thought that there were three cats too many. He didn't pay attention to them. He didn't talk to them. He merely acted like they weren't there. At first Mariana thought the cats' charming ways would win Thomas over, but that never happened.

One day, Thomas came home from work and Mariana knew he had had a bad day. He stomped around the apartment and growled when she asked him what was wrong. He fixed himself a drink and then another drink. Instead of becoming mellow, he became belligerent. One of the cats, Brinkley, accidentally got in the way of Thomas' stomping and Thomas kicked the cat. Brinkley went flying across the room and landed in a heap, stunned. Mariana was aghast.

She went running over to her cat and picked him up and cradled him in her arms. Mariana could tell that he was hurt and packed him up right away and took him to the emergency clinic which was open after normal hours. It was determined that Brinkley had several broken ribs which had to be bound close to his body. After much angst and fewer dollars in Mariana's purse, she took Brinkley home and put him in a room by himself. She was so appalled by this act of cruelty she couldn't even look at Thomas. His behavior was so unacceptable she didn't have the words she needed at the time to even speak to him.

That night she slept in the room with Brinkley. Things went downhill quickly after that. Shortly thereafter, she told Thomas to leave and that she wanted a divorce. He seemed relieved and it didn't take him long to find an apartment across town. The divorce was granted, and since there were no children involved it was legally uncomplicated for Mariana and Thomas to part ways.

Mariana stayed in the apartment with the three cats. Brinkley recovered from his broken ribs and lived a long and happy life. The other two cats seemed more at ease without the hulking presence of Thomas. Mariana lavished attention on all three. She was happy living with her furry babies and they blossomed under her tender care. The years went on and she acquired a few more cats and some of the original ones passed away peacefully, usually from old age maladies. She sometimes volunteered at the local shelter, specializing in cats, of course. She would groom the cats and help with clean up. She was devoted to cats and never found another man to live with. Cats filled her life.

As she drove toward the grocery store, she wondered why she was thinking about Thomas. They didn't keep in touch and she hardly ever saw him, which was just fine with her. The hurt of his meanness to Brinkley stayed with her for a long time. She pushed the image of him out of her mind and turned into the hot parking lot.

A flash of white ran across the lot and Mariana slammed on her brakes. Was that a cat? A white cat? She didn't see it but she parked the car and walked over to where she had thought it was. She looked under a few cars but didn't see any cat. She thought it must have been her imagination so she continued into the store to do her shopping. After about an hour she exited the store and began loading the groceries into the car's trunk. Continuing to look around the parking lot, she thought she saw a flick of a white tail underneath a car in a row over from her car. Mariana was sweating from the intense heat and she deliberately walked toward the white splotch that was moving slowly on the hot pavement. Arriving at the car, she bent down and saw a large all-white cat peering out from around a tire.

"Oh, you poor thing! What are you doing out here?" she asked the cat. "It's so hot your paws must be burning up! Come on out so I can see you."

The cat didn't move. "Ok, let me try an old trick. You stay there and I'll be right back." Mariana went to her car and opened the trunk and took out a can of cat food. She opened it and walked back to where the white cat was still hiding. A couple came out of the grocery store and stared at her.

"There's a cat under this car and I want to try to get him out of there," she told them. The people moved away without saying anything.

She put the can of food down on the pavement close to the tire and backed away a few feet to watch. The white cat sniffed the air and zeroed in on the can. Tentatively the cat came forward and began to eat the food out of the can.

"I don't want you to eat it all and lick the can because the insides are sharp and you might cut your tongue," Mariana warned the cat. The cat scarfed down the beef and chicken dinner hungrily and didn't seem to pay much attention to the warning.

Mariana reached out to take the can away and as she was doing so, the white cat sniffed her hand.

"You're not a feral cat; you must belong to someone." The cat just looked at her and took a small step closer.

"I won't hurt you.   Come out so I can see you." Taking small steps, the cat walked out into the bright sunshine and came up to Mariana and looked into her eyes.

Mariana put her hand on the cat's back and it arched into her touch. "You're a very pretty cat. Why are you here? Where are your owners?" The cat didn't answer but merely let the friendly hand stroke her.

Just at that time, a large woman came toward the car and popped open the trunk. The sound scared the cat, who ran back under the car to hide.

Mariana said, "Is this your cat?" The woman stared at Mariana like she had lost her mind.

"What cat?"

"This one that is under your car."

The woman labored to bend down to take a look. "That's not my cat. I don't have any cats and I don't need any."

"Well, this one was out here in the hot parking lot and ran under your car."

"I'm sorry, but the cat doesn't belong to me. I need to put these groceries in the car and get home now."

"How about the cat?"

"I don't know. I don't really like cats, so I guess he belongs to you now unless you can find out who owns him. Or you could just leave him here. That would be the easiest thing to do."

"Oh my. Maybe I can go back into the store and see if they'll make an announcement that there is a cat in the parking lot," Mariana told her.

"Well, you can try that. I really need to leave now." She sat down in the driver's seat and started the car, which scared the cat, who ran underneath another car.

Mariana was unsure of what to do.

She told the cat, "Ok, you stay right here and I'll be back in a few minutes." She walked back into the store and asked to speak to the manager. The manager was paged and a tall thin man wearing a starched white shirt appeared after a few minutes. His name tag read, 'Mr. Rob Dolenz, Assistant Manager.'

"What can I do for you, ma'am?" he asked.

"There's a cat out in the parking lot. Maybe he belongs to someone in the store."

The assistant manager looked at Mariana trying to size her up and reluctantly said, "What do you want me to do?"

"Could you get on the loudspeaker and see if the cat's owner is in the store? It is so hot outside and the cat is just running from underneath one car to another. I feel so sorry for him."

"Do you mean that there's a stray cat outside and you want me to interrupt our customers' shopping experience with this information?"

"Well, yes I guess I do. It's about 95 degrees outside and the poor cat is exhausted and very hot. I think it's the least you could do." Then she added, "I shop in this store almost every week and I'd appreciate it if you'd do this one favor."

Mr. Dolenz shifted his weight from foot to foot and glanced around. "This is probably against store policy and that's not really the way we handle these things, but I guess I could do it this one time."

"That would be good."

"I'm a dog man myself and there are so many stray cats around I don't pay much attention to them."

"Mr. Dolenz, this white cat is no stray and he's suffering. Someone is going to run over him with their car if you don't do something about it."

"That would be bad publicity for the store and then it might make me look bad. I'll make an announcement one time to see if someone shows up."

"Thank you," Mariana responded.

Mr. Dolenz picked up a microphone and quickly said, "There's a white cat in the parking lot. If he belongs to anyone, please come to the front of the store so you can retrieve him." His tinny voice resounded throughout the store.

Mariana thought briefly about her own groceries that were melting in the trunk of her car, but watched the people coming and going to see if anyone would claim the white cat. Dog man Dolenz stalked off to attend to the canned beans and carrots. After about 10 or 15 minutes no one had come forward, so Mariana went back outside to look for the cat. To her surprise, the cat had stationed itself at the door and perked up when Mariana came out.

"Ok, let's go. You can't stay here and it looks like whoever left you isn't coming back."

Mariana picked up the white cat and carried him to her car. As she placed the cat on the front seat, the cat turned around and Mariana exclaimed, "Why, you're not a male; you're a female!"

"Yes, I am definitely that," the cat thought to herself.

IVORY

Many days had passed since Kitty had been adopted from the shelter. Time seemed to slow down and Ivory moped in her cage. She didn't want to go to the playroom or interact with the other cats. Lounging in the back of the cage, not many adopters glanced her way as they scanned the room full of cats. She thought that she would just spend the rest of her days behind bars, watching the world go past. Her friend was gone and she was depressed. Her thick fur began to thin out and the luster in her eyes became a dull glaze. She lost weight and didn't take an interest in the food they brought two times a day. Ivory began to look like a cat who was years older, not the vibrant one whose personality shined brightly when Kitty was around. The gentle cat was becoming a recluse.

Then one slow day, a young man came in the room. He was in his 20s with a few discreet tattoos, one of which was a butterfly. His clothes were average and he had close-cropped dark hair and a shadow of a beard. Stopping in the doorway and looking around at all the caged cats he sort of sighed. Some of the cats took notice but most of them were napping. He was holding a cardboard box with air holes in it, which was the kind used to transport cats if one didn't have a proper cage. The man gave the impression that he meant to take a cat home with him.

Walking around the room, he began looking into the cages. It was hard to decide what he was thinking or what type of cat he was looking for. His demeanor was restrained but his eyes were roving quickly around the room, as if he wanted to get a cat and get out of there but didn't want to give the impression that he was in a hurry. He went up to a cage full of rambunctious kittens. Four 3 month old black and white kittens shared the same cage and were tumbling and play fighting with each other. He smiled briefly and then moved on. He gradually made his way over to Ivory's cage where he paused and set the cage down.

"Hi there. So you're Ivory, huh? I can see that the name fits you well. My name is Steve. How would you like to go home with me?"

Ivory didn't make a move from her retreat in the back of the cage. She thought to herself that there was something not quite right with the way he acted but she couldn't put her paw on it. There was no particular reason why he would choose her unless he was just looking for a pure white cat. She wasn't very pretty anymore and she wasn't even that friendly.

Steve put his fingers in the cage and wiggled them. Ivory just looked at him.

"Let's see if we can take you out so I can look at you better," he told her. Steve went out to find a volunteer and came back within a minute with the person on duty. She opened Ivory's cage and let Steve hold her. Ivory squirmed a bit but didn't put up a big fuss.

"Ivory has been losing weight and has not been herself ever since her cat friend was adopted," the volunteer told Steve.

"Well, I can see that she must have been pretty at one time. Maybe I can help her get back to her old self." Ivory looked up at Steve and still had an uneasy feeling. What was it about him that she didn't like?

"Let's pack her up so I can take her home," he said. Everything was happening so fast, Ivory didn't have time to think. She'd be leaving her cage where she had spent many months. She wouldn't be living at the shelter anymore. She was going to a place where she had never been before with a man she didn't really like. Ivory was helpless to do anything about it. The volunteer placed Ivory in the cardboard carrier. She looked through the air holes and the cats who were watching her stared back. As she put her paw through the hole it was almost as if she was sadly waving goodbye. A few of the other cats meowed softly their goodbyes.

The paperwork was completed at the front desk and Ivory was taken outside to an older model car and put in the back seat. Steve didn't talk to her as he drove away from the shelter. She meowed several times, but he didn't acknowledge her. Ivory put her paw through a hole but there was nothing to grab so she settled down in the carrier to await her fate.

About a half hour later, Steve drove into a parking lot.

He parked the car and said, "I'll be back in a few minutes." He cracked open a window a few inches in the front seat to allow some air in and got out of the car. The air-conditioning wasn't working very well and it was already warm in the back seat. Ivory looked out through the holes and saw other cars in the parking lot. She could tell it was hot outside...very hot. The asphalt seemed to be almost melting in the heat. It was too hot to trot. The car started heating up quickly. Ivory began to pant. With her pink tongue hanging out of her mouth, she was a pitiful sight if anyone could have seen her.

She also began to panic. "Let meooowwtt! It's hot in here!"

The sun beat down on the car's roof and magnified its intensity in the car's interior. Ivory thought she might have a heat stroke before Steve returned. She started to tear at the air holes in the carrier but didn't make much headway. She became frantic which increased her body temperature. Being clothed in a fur coat didn't help at all either. She had to get out of there! Some people passed the car on their way into the store but didn't look her way. She meowed and meowed but no one heard her. She thought if she had been a dog, she could have barked and maybe someone might have noticed her but no one could hear her voice.

The heat was becoming unbearable. Ivory ripped at the holes and shreds of cardboard fell on the back seat. Without claws it was hard to get a grip. Finally she began to push on the top of the carrier with her head to see if it would open from the top. It was locked together but it started to move upward a bit. If only she was strong enough to get it open….in her weakened condition she thought it was unlikely she would be able to escape, but she had to keep trying. Ivory gave one big push and at last the top of the carrier broke free and she could look up at the inside roof of the car. With one motion, she jumped out of the carrier and into the front seat. It seemed to be even hotter there and she thought she might die. The leather seats burned her paws. But then she saw the window that was down a few inches. She HAD to get out of there and the window was her only escape route. She looked around the lot for Steve but didn't see him. So she started to wiggle her thin body out through the window opening. Cats know how to get in and out of tight places and the opening wasn't much but she pushed herself and squeezed her body through the window and briefly hung onto the outside of the window and then dropped to the ground. She was exhausted by the effort but at least she was out of the death trap. She became aware of the scorching black asphalt that was melting in patches and burning her pads. A bird would have to use potholders to pull a worm out of the ground, it was that hot. Scooting under the car didn't help much because it was still burning her feet. Where to go? What to do? Wait for Steve to come back? Risk running through the parking lot and getting run over? Ivory's head hurt and her body hurt. She needed some water but there wasn't any available.

As she was catching her breath and trying to breathe normally, she could see the feet and legs of people passing. Her thought processes began to recover and she started to think a bit more clearly. She was in a precarious position she knew, but maybe she could improve her chances. She knew she didn't like Steve and felt uncomfortable with him. She still couldn't decide why he had chosen her and why it had all happened so quickly but her sharp cat instincts told her to get away from him. So, she looked around for him and still didn't see him and ran underneath a few cars away from his car. Ow! Oww! Ouch! The pavement was blistering her feet! She saw the store ahead but there were a lot of people going in and coming out with carts full of groceries that she decided to stay put for a while. Still miserable from the hot parking lot, she tried to hide behind a car's tire. She was ill-concealed being all white but there was nothing she could do about that.

Then she saw him come out of the store carrying a bag full of groceries. He headed toward his car and put the bag into the trunk. Opening the driver's side door, she could see him look in the back seat where the empty cat carrier was. He began to search under the seats and under the dashboard area, but of course, Ivory wasn't there. Steve then looked around the parking lot and Ivory hid herself as best she could behind the car's tire. Steve was sweating and looked irritated and mumbled a few curse words. He walked around a bit and bent down to look under a few cars but soon he gave up and climbed into his car. Steve drove away. Ivory breathed a bit easier, but she wasn't out of the woods (or the parking lot) yet.

A big truck rumbled down the pavement close to her hiding place and it scared her. Ivory knew she couldn't stay in this spot for long, so she made a run for it. A car slammed on the brakes and stopped. The woman driver quickly zeroed in on her but Ivory ran in the opposite direction, again taking shelter under a car. She watched as the woman parked her car and started to look around. Ivory laid low and tried to think rationally. The woman shrugged and walked into the store to do her shopping. A few more people came out of the store and loaded their groceries into their cars. Luckily, the car she was hiding under wasn't moved. Ivory was worn out. She was really thirsty and she was extremely tired but she couldn't just take a nap on the hot asphalt. So she suffered in silence.

After a while, Ivory noticed the same lady come out of the store and put groceries into her car. All of a sudden the lady walked toward Ivory and began to talk to her. Ivory meowed faintly in response. The lady went to her car and lo and behold, took out a can of cat food from the car's trunk, opened it and put it in front of Ivory's face. Oh, it smelled so good! The white cat quickly ate the food while the lady watched her. She had a kind face and Ivory could tell she was a cat person. The lady walked back into the store which puzzled Ivory. After a few minutes she didn't come out and Ivory decided to chance it and looked around carefully before scampering quickly toward the front door of the store. She positioned herself so she could see who was coming out. A few people stopped when they saw her and one or two talked to her and petted her. Ivory wasn't afraid anymore since she had seen Steve drive away. She just waited close to the door as if she knew this would be her destiny.

JAZMINE

Kitty awoke to the sound of scraping and clicking. She was momentarily afraid at the unfamiliar sound and tried to squirm under the quilt, but then she saw Buster limping in the door and she relaxed. His toenails had been clicking on the floor and he was dragging his back legs as he moved. He slowly made his way over to the edge of the bed and rested his head on the side to gaze at Kitty.

"Are you ok?" he asked her. "You've been asleep for quite a while."

Kitty stretched out her paw and touched him on the nose. "Yeah, I was just tired and the bed was so soft and inviting."

Buster tried to sit down, but his legs wouldn't cooperate and he sort of fell into a heap on the floor. He looked worn out and uncomfortable. "Oh, I know about being tired," he said. "One of these days I probably won't be able to get up and then it will be my time to go."

"Don't say that!" Kitty exclaimed. "You may have more time than you think. No one knows when his time is up, but you just have to live each day to its fullest. Your body may be wearing out but your mind is still active and you have a nice home here and Monique loves you. You've had a good life."

"But I think everyone has to accept that at some point they are going to die. No one lives forever. I just wish that I had more time to do some other things."

"What would you like to do if you could?" Kitty asked him.

Buster thought a moment and then said, "I'd like to go to the beach again. I want to run into the surf and swim in the ocean and play with a Frisbee on the sand. I want to lie next to Monique under an umbrella and shake the water out of my fur. I want to run up and down the beach and catch a ball and play tag with it as it drifts out in the ocean."

"Sounds like you've had some experience with those things."

"I love the beach. It's been a few years since Monique took me but the memories are still vivid in my mind. Have you ever been to the beach?"

"No, I haven't but it doesn't sound that appealing to me. The hot sand would probably burn my paw pads and I would be scared of the sound of the ocean waves. But, the sand sure would make a good litter box!"

Buster sort of chuckled. "I'd also like to go to a dog park again. I'd be able to meet a whole new group of dog friends and we could play together. There would be plenty of room to run around and I would feel care-free and easy. But those dreams are out of my reach now. I can't run anymore and Monique probably thinks I wouldn't enjoy the beach as much as I used to."

"But they're your dreams…..you can think about them and almost imagine that you are at the beach or at the dog park. It wouldn't be quite the same thing, but it would be a pleasant way to remember the good times you had. Maybe we can think of some way to get Monique to take you to the beach one more time."

"How would we do that?" Buster inquired.

"I don't know but let me think about it." Kitty stretched and jumped down from the bed and landed beside Buster. "Can I help you get up?" she asked him.

"No, I can still get up; it may take a while but I can make it," he replied. He turned his rump around so it was higher than his forelegs and sort of pushed himself up into a standing position. He followed Kitty into the kitchen and then into the utility room.

"I think Monique must have gone to the store to get some cat food while you were asleep."

"Well, that's always a good thing," Kitty remarked. She walked over to the litter box and scratched in the sand-like litter. The litter felt good to her paws and then an idea came to her.

"Buster! Come over here!" He ambled toward the litter box.

"Look, I'm going to scratch some of this litter onto the floor. When we hear Monique coming, I want you to lie down in it and try to roll over on your back and act like you're at the beach. Can you do that?"

"Well, I can try. It won't be very easy for me to roll over but maybe I can lie down and scoot over on it."

"Do you think she'll get the hint? Or do you think she'll just be upset that I threw the litter on the floor?"

"Monique doesn't get upset at what we do. She's pretty easy-going. As to whether she'll know what I want…..we'll just have to see what happens."

So Buster and Kitty waited side by side, looking out the window that faced the parking area. Presently they saw Monique's car pull up and park. She opened the trunk and took out a large bag, shut the trunk and locked her car. She began to walk toward the building. Kitty jumped up and went over to the litter box and began scratching the litter furiously onto the floor. When a good pile was made, she beckoned to Buster to come over. He painfully slid down next to the litter and flopped over on his side.

"Can you put your paws up in the air before she gets here?" Kitty asked him.

"Sort of. It hurts to try to stretch them out." But he did and Kitty approved of his position. Buster actually looked like he was having fun and he had a comical look on his old face. They heard the turning of the key in the lock and expectantly looked toward the door. Monique came through the door and immediately saw the strange scene in the corner of the room. An old black dog upside down moving around in a pile of cat litter and the new cat silently looking on.

"What is going on here with you two? Why is there litter all over the floor? And Buster, what do you think you're doing there?" Buster moved from side to side on his back imitating playing at the beach. Monique just stood there stock still taking in the bizarre action. She put the bag of food down and walked over to the dog and knelt down next to him. She regarded him with a quizzical expression. Buster smiled up at her.

"I haven't seen you play like this for a long time. It reminds me of the last time I took you to the beach. Does the litter make you think of being at the beach?" Buster moved around on his back to indicate his affirmative answer. Kitty brushed up against Monique's arm and she took notice of the little calico.

"You're a silly cat, little one." Kitty was impressed that Monique caught on so quickly to their little scheme.

As Monique was putting away the cat food, she looked over her shoulder at Buster and said, "Maybe we should go to the beach one day this weekend. What do you think?"

Buster barked an affirmative answer.

"Ok, we'll leave early on Saturday morning. I think Kitty can stay here by herself for the day, right Kitty?" Kitty rubbed up against her leg as Monique began to sweep up all the cat litter.

Things went well for me as I settled into Monique's home and developed a friendship with Buster. Monique took Buster to the beach for the day and they both enjoyed it immensely. When they returned from their outing, Buster told me all about his adventure:

"I could walk in the sand. I'm not able to run anymore, but the sand helped to steady my legs without a hard surface. It was a perfect day to be at the beach; it was not too hot or too cool. Monique put up the umbrella close to the surf so we would have some shade from the sun. I took a few steps into the water and it was just as wonderful as I remembered it. As I was lying at the water's edge a wave broke over me and I was drenched. I loved it! I stayed there for a long time as Monique read her book. She brought along a little dish and some bottled water for me so I wouldn't get dehydrated. I thought about old times when I could run through the surf and chase a small beach ball into the waves. Such fond memories I had! I'm so glad that you thought of how to show Monique that I wanted to go back to the beach. Thank you for that."

"Well, I'm just glad to help. That's great that you had such a good time," I told him.

"Now Monique has to wash me in the tub because I have salt in my fur."

"That doesn't sound like much fun," I replied.

"I don't mind it at all."

I was reminded of the vast differences between cats and dogs. I didn't have much exposure to water but I knew I probably wouldn't like it. A cat is not a dog!

Monique went to work almost every day. I found out that she worked in a beauty salon, doing peoples' hair and nails. She always left the house dressed well and immaculately groomed. Her dark hair was styled and she moved with the grace of a cat. I could tell she worked hard and was standing on her feet most of the day because the first thing Monique did when she came home was to kick off her shoes.

Monique was also a social person who liked to party. Some nights she would leave the house after feeding Buster and me and not return until after midnight. I thought she should get more sleep, but Monique seemed to fare well with only a few hours of rest. Not me! I liked to sleep many hours during the day and most of the night. Sometimes I would get the "kitten crazies" and just run around the house, up and over the furniture, onto the chair and table and look down at Buster who would just shake his head in perplexity. I was just running off some of my energy, a thing I hadn't been able to do in my previous homes. At times I would sleep close to Buster because he made a nice pillow to prop on. He didn't mind at all.

A few weeks later, Monique planned to host a party at the house. Both Buster and I knew about it because she had been on the phone inviting her friends over. Monique brought home party food and drinks and began preparing some hors d'oeurves.

Buster told me, "It's best that we find a place that's out of the way because sometimes Monique's friends aren't as savvy about dogs and cats as she is and we don't want to be stepped on or worse."

We decided that we would spend the time during the party in the back bedroom, in a corner so maybe no one would notice us. Party time came and the guests began arriving. I could hear people moving around in the front part of the apartment, laughing and having a good time. I wasn't afraid of people, but I wasn't quite sure I wanted to meet all these strangers, so I just kept myself partially hidden next to Buster. The music cranked up and I knew it wasn't classical music, which I preferred. I got up and peeked around the door and saw about 20 people of all different ages and types. Monique's friends were sure a lively bunch. One woman with long black hair and a startling red outfit was dancing in the middle of the floor by herself while a few others looked on. Most people were standing around talking with drinks in their hands. The dancing woman happened to glance in my direction and kept staring at me. I backed off into the bedroom again and retreated to Buster's side. I didn't like being stared at, especially by someone I didn't know.

The dark haired woman walked into the room and spied us in the corner. She then moved slowly toward me and Buster and knelt down beside us. She stroked Buster's fur and extended her hand to me. I sniffed it and acknowledged that she didn't mean any harm. The woman smelled like beer but it wasn't overwhelming or unpleasant.

"I know Buster, but I haven't seen you, little kitten. You must be new here," she said to me. She touched me on the head and I looked at her warily.

Just then, Monique came into the room and saw her friend kneeling on the floor.

"How do you like my new kitten, Kitty?" she asked her friend.

"Kitty! Is that her name?" the woman exclaimed.

"She was given that name before I adopted her, Trina."

Trina gazed at me and said, "I think she deserves another name. Something more suited to her personality. Something jazzy. Monique, don't you want her to have another, more appropriate name?"

"Well, I had thought about it but hadn't come up with just the right name yet."

"Let's see. She seems to like the music. How about Jazzy?"

"No, I can't quite see her as a Jazzy," Monique said.

"Ok, what about Jazmine with a 'z'?"

Monique considered it, looking thoughtfully at me.

"What do you think, Kitty? Are you a Jazmine?"

I sure didn't feel like a Jazmine, but I didn't say anything.

Monique told Trina, "I sort of like it. She kind of looks like a Jazmine."

Trina said, "Well, Jazmine it is."

And that is how I became Jazmine.

Buster snickered from his corner as the two women left the room. "Jazmine!" he said.

I sighed. The naming of cats confounded me. The name "Jazmine" conjured up images of a worldly cat, prone to living in high style in a big city. I was just a kitten, living my life with an old dog and a nice lady in an apartment. How did people name their pets anyway? My first name, "Kitty" was just a generic name given to me by my first family. They didn't really care about me and gave me a convenient name that could apply to any number of cats. I felt it didn't really suit me; I had more personality than a "Kitty" did. Cat names are like people names in that trends set the tone. Owners find inspiration in human baby names since cats are now considered family members. Using adjectives for names seems to be passé, like Whitey,

Smokey, Mittens, or Snowball. No one really named their cats Felix or Tabby or Frisky anymore, just like people didn't name their little girls Betty, Susie or Judy like they did years ago. Instead popular girls' names were those like Madison, Caitlin, and Brianna. Many boys' names tended to remain the same throughout the years although most people don't name their dogs Spot, Rover or Blackie anymore. I sighed again and decided to make the best of it.

The party wound down way past midnight as the last of the stragglers finally went home. Buster and I made our way into the living room to see lots of paper plates, glasses, bottles and cans littering the floor and tables. The leftover food smelled good to me and Buster and then Monique gave us each some tidbits from the table.

"Jazmine! How do you like your new name?" Monique asked me.

I gave her an indifferent look.

"You'll get used to it eventually. I think it rather suits you. Trina did you a favor."

I thought, "Right. But I guess it's better than 'Kitty.'"

BUSTER

I settled into my new life easily. Remembering my friend Ivory, I thought about how much I missed her and hoped that someone had adopted her. I tried not to dwell on those thoughts because it still made me sad. I spent most of my days keeping Buster company and waiting for Monique to come home. I would always greet Monique at the door, rubbing against her and looking expectantly up, hoping for a bit of attention. Monique would change clothes and get down on the floor with Buster and me, petting us and telling us about her day at the salon. She would then usually feed us and herself and then sometimes go out for the evening. I began sleeping next to Buster in his dog bed. We both enjoyed each other's company and were comfortable with the fact that I was a cat and he was a dog. I thought there was no reason for cats and dogs not to get along; it was just that some people taught their dogs that cats were prey and the dogs behaved accordingly.

I could tell that Buster was slowing down gradually day by day. To help keep his spirits up, I asked him about his life and the things he had done over the years. Buster had been a "throw away" when he was a puppy. Abandoned in the woods as a youngster by people who didn't want him, he had wandered for several days through thickets of trees and dense shrubs, trying to find something to eat and drink. It was difficult because he was so young and didn't have the hunting skills necessary to survive in the woods. After a few days he came upon a cliff that dropped away steeply to a river many feet below him. Buster timidly looked over the edge and saw that there was no way he could ever make his way down to the water. He backed away and ran to and fro along the edge. A few stones tumbled down and he could hear them splash in the river water far below. His thirst was fierce and his throat was parched and the sound of the running water made him even more thirsty. Oh, just to have a long drink of cool, refreshing water! What could he do? He lay down panting and peered over the cliff. He barked softly but no one could hear him. Was he just going to die there on the edge?

All of a sudden, he saw a shadow moving over the greenery and looked up to see a big black hawk circling. Or maybe it was a buzzard? The bird's beady eyes zeroed in on Buster and the puppy tried to hide underneath some low-growing vegetation, but he had been spotted already. In his weakened condition, he had few options. The dark shadow came around again, but a bit closer this time. Buster tried to scrunch his body under the shrub, but his black fur was like a beacon to the predator. He could see the talons and knew that they could pick up a little dog like him very easily. He could jump over the cliff, but what chance would he have then, landing in the water and probably drowning? He could try to run back the way he had come, but the bird would just follow him. Buster moaned a little puppy sound.

It was then he heard a distant motor on the river below. He scrambled out from under the bush and again gazed over the edge where he saw a fishing boat slowly making its way down the river, close to the bank. There were three people in the boat casting their lines toward the bank and reeling them in as the boat coasted lazily in the current.

Buster barked as loud as he could. The hawk/buzzard took notice and swooped down several feet above the puppy's head. Buster barked again and again. The black menace circled around and took a nose dive at the little dog, grazing his back. Ouch! That hurt! Buster knew the next time would be his last, being grabbed with those sharp claws, lifted up into the air and then either dropped or taken away to become a tasty dinner. Buster barked one more time.

The people in the boat finally heard what they thought was a bird's cry and looked upward. Way up on the cliff they all saw a dark shape close to the edge and a menacing black bird diving down. One of the people shouted at the raptor and reluctantly it flew away to find another morsel for its dinner.

One of the men in the boat began to climb up the sheer face of the cliff, finding footholds and branches to cling to as he pulled his way up. After what seemed like an interminably long time, he finally reached the top and was astonished to see the little black pup wagging his tail in front of him.

"What the heck are you doing up here all by yourself?" he asked Buster.

Buster just ran back and forth with joy at being rescued.

"How did you get out here in the wilderness? There aren't any houses around for miles."

"And now, how are we going to get you down to the boat?"

Buster didn't know; he was just glad to see the man with wavy red hair. The man grinned at him and picked him up.

"You're no bigger than a peanut. That old hawk would have made short work of you."

The man put Buster in his plaid jacket and zipped it up so Buster was secure and not able to fall out. Gingerly, the man began to climb backwards down the face of the cliff, back toward the boat. Both of the other people continued to watch this spectacle from the boat, their fishing gear forgotten. "Red" finally put his foot on the spare and rocky ground beneath the cliff and the other foot in the boat.

"Look what I found!" he said to his companions as he unzipped his jacket. Buster tumbled out and wagged his tail.

"Wow!" said a woman, one of the people who was fishing. "How did he get up there?"

Red said, "I don't know, but there is no civilization around for miles. I'll bet he's hungry and thirsty."

The other older man picked through a cooler and found a plastic dish and poured some bottled water into it. He also found a sandwich which he tore into small pieces. He put the sandwich on a bag on the bottom of the boat along with the water. Buster gobbled it down and drank the entire dish of water.

The man said, "Look, he's starving. He probably hasn't eaten in days."

"What are we going to do with him?" asked the woman.

"Well, it's obvious he doesn't belong to anyone, way out here by himself."

"Since he's eaten and had a drink, let's keep on fishing for a while," she said.

"Ok. Sounds good."

Buster, feeling much better, found a spot close to the older man's feet and curled up. He looked up at the man and the man smiled down at him. "He's a cute little thing, even if he is an orphan."

The people fished for a while longer and then took the boat back to the area where the truck was parked and pulled the boat up onto the trailer. Buster stayed in the back seat with Red on the drive home.

The three people and the dog drove about ten minutes and pulled up to a house on a hill that overlooked the same river from which Buster had been rescued. Buster scrambled out of the truck and immediately began exploring and sniffing the ground. Two dogs ran out to greet the people and regarded Buster carefully. One dog, a large black lab and the other, a three-legged mix of indeterminate parentage circled little Buster and rubbed noses with him. A lot of sniffing took place and it was decided that everyone could get along peacefully. Several cats also were checking out Buster from afar.

The little dog spent a few nights at the fisherman's house sleeping in the basement with the two resident dogs. It just so happened that at that time Monique, who was about ten years old, lived next door to these people. Monique lived with her mother and a big orange cat with long hair. One day, she came over to visit and fell in love with Buster. She asked her neighbors if they were going to keep him and they told her they already had enough pets, but if she would ask her mother, they would be willing to give Buster to her. Things worked out so that the next day Buster moved in with Monique, her mother and the orange cat. He lived in the house on the hill and spent his life with Monique, even after she had grown up and moved into her own apartment. He continued to be friends with his two dog neighbors and even with the multitude of cats who lived there. The three dogs could often be seen together, traveling down a well-worn path that led to the river's edge. They would splash in the water and chase each other and climb back up to the top of the hill wet, tired and happy. This went on for many years until the older dogs could no longer climb the hill, especially the three-legged one. "Tripod" had lost his front leg to a rattlesnake when he was very young. The snake had bitten him and his humans had to have the leg amputated, but he got along very well without it. He compensated and limped, but he was still active and loved to wrestle with the other dogs.

So, even though little Buster had a not so good beginning in life, the rest of it was very satisfactory. He loved Monique and couldn't imagine living anywhere else. Buster and the orange cat got along well together, too. Now he knew that he would soon be crossing the rainbow bridge, but he had led a comfortable and happy life and if that's not enough for a dog, what is?

He told me other stories about his growing up years, especially ones that involved going to the beach. He was still so pleased that he had been able to visit the beach one last time, due to my cleverness with the litter box trick. Buster and I grew to be close friends as the months passed. Buster became weaker and less able to move about. As I watched Buster day by day, I was disturbed at the thought of losing my friend. I tried to help him whenever I could, but I was so tiny compared to Buster, there wasn't much I could do.

Several months passed and all seemed peaceful and quiet. Then one day, Buster cried out, "I can't get up! What will I do? My legs won't hold me up anymore. How will I go outside?" I was alarmed at this development and tried to think logically. Monique happened to be home at the time and I quickly strode over to her and began to scratch her pants, like I was sharpening my claws. Since I had never done this before, Monique looked at me quizzically and asked, "What are you doing? You know where the scratching post is."

I ran back to where Buster was lying on his side near his bed. I then ran back to Monique. "What's wrong? Is there something wrong with Buster?" I ran back to Buster's side. Buster groaned softly. Monique knelt down beside Buster and cradled his head in her arms. "What's the matter, old boy? Do you hurt somewhere?"

She reached out to touch Buster's front leg and he winced and pulled it back.

"Uh oh," she whispered. "What are we going to do now?" Tears started to fall on Buster's black fur. Monique cried quietly while I looked on. I rubbed up against Monique's arms and back and wrapped my tail around Monique in an attempt to try to comfort her. I laid a soft paw on Monique's brown arm and gazed up at her with love in my eyes. Stroking me, Monique held Buster's head and looked into his eyes, which were still alert but reflected the pain he was feeling. Buster was too heavy for Monique to carry up and down the stairs when he had to go outside and both of them knew it. There would be no way for him to function when he was so crippled that he was unable to walk.

"Ohhh," Buster said. "I'll probably never be able to walk again. My body is failing me but my mind is still quick. I can see fairly well and my hearing isn't what it used to be and I still have an appetite, even though I've lost some weight. I'm alive but without the use of my legs, I might as well be dead."

"Oh, please don't say that!" I cried. "Maybe Monique can think of something to do."

"There's nothing that can be done for me. I can't go up and down the stairs anymore."

I was so depressed at this thought that I went up to Buster and tried to massage his legs with my paws. Buster winced but knew I was trying to help him. He put his head on his front paws and looked up into my eyes.

He said, "Thank you for being such a good friend to me. I really needed a companion and Monique couldn't have chosen a better one than you. I know I won't be around much longer, but I don't want you to be sad when I go. You are young and have many years ahead of you and many more adventures to experience. Maybe Monique will even take you to the beach," he teased me.

"I don't want to go to the beach! I want you to stay here with me!"

"I can't. I've used up all my nine lives, if dogs have nine lives like cats do. We just both have to accept the inevitable."

"Oh! My friend and buddy........what will I do without you?"

"You will stay here and enjoy your life with Monique. There couldn't be a better housemate than Monique. Years from now we'll meet again over the rainbow bridge."

"The rainbow bridge! I can't bear to think about it." I rubbed up against Buster's face and purred in his ear.

Monique had picked up her cell phone and was dialing the number of the veterinarian. She spoke quietly into the phone and relayed all that had happened. There was a short conversation that Buster and I couldn't hear, but when she hung up, she was crying again. She walked over to Buster and said, "Sweet dog, I'm afraid that there's not much that I can do for you now. Rather than put you through the indignity of what we both know will happen, I've asked Dr. Dean to come over after work today. I'm so sorry! We're going to have to say goodbye sooner than I thought." Monique continued to sob into Buster's fur.

Oh, so soon, I thought. Too soon! My little cat heart was hurting just from the thought of having to say goodbye to my loyal friend. I snuggled up closer to Buster and licked his paw.

Buster painfully put his paw over Monique's arm and the dog, the woman and I lay in a heap on the floor awaiting the knock on the door.

The knock came about an hour later and Monique got up to answer it. Dr. Dean came in the room and knelt down by Buster. She looked in his eyes, took out her stethoscope and listened to his heartbeat and tried to manipulate his legs and paws. Buster cried out in pain.

The vet said to Monique, "It's time. We could give him some pain medication but we'd just be postponing it and he'd still be suffering. Are you ready? Take all the time you need."

Monique cried out, "No I'm not ready but I don't want him to suffer. I'd rather suffer than see Buster suffer. Go ahead."

Dr. Dean removed some instruments from her bag. She shaved a small place on Buster's front arm and used a sanitary wipe to cleanse the area.

I thought I could not watch this and tried to turn away but Monique was holding me with her free arm and I didn't want to cause Monique any more distress. Oh how sad! The black dog looked back and forth at me and Monique.

"I'll miss you, Jazmine. I was so lucky that you came into my life. You were the best friend a dog could have, even if you are a cat."

"Buster! I love you! I'll never forget you."

"I love you too, sweet one."

The vet inserted the needle into Buster's arm and squeezed the liquid into his vein. Buster laid his head on Monique's lap and in a second he was gone.

REMEMBERING ROMEO

The temperatures were getting progressively colder each day. Most of the leaves had already fallen to the damp ground in the woods except for a few stubborn brown ones that clung to some old gnarly oaks. The skies had turned a casket gray and I knew that before long the snow and cold would come. I knew what it would be like since I had spent winters outside and it was nothing to look forward to. I dreaded the bone-chilling cold when there was no place to warm up. My fur had thickened somewhat in anticipation of the coming winter, but it was still no substitute for a nice warm lap or a place beside a heater. There were a few rough patchy spots in my coat where I had scratched myself in the summer. My skin was so raw that I had bled. The fleas were so bad I felt like I was being consumed by them and in a way I was because the little blood suckers were depleting my energy. There was no escaping the fleas. They multiplied on me like a rabbit having babies, but so many more. Fleas were nasty but they were a fact of life in the warm months when one is in the woods.

I had not seen the chainsaw man since I had rescued him. I had heard, however, gunshots periodically and that scared me. Imagining that hunters were prowling around the woods made me shiver. They might mistake me for a fox and my speed was no match for bullets. The crisp fall leaves crunched under my feet as I picked my way gingerly through a pathway that had probably been made by deer.

I needed to find something to eat but I was tired. My body felt old even though I wasn't old. I was approaching the prime of my life but most of my energy had to be concentrated on staying alive, eating and avoiding predators. I began questioning my choice to run away and live on my own instead of living with a person. Was this the wisest move? Probably not, but I had been tired of having decisions made for me that affected my life. The alternative would be that I could leave the woods, find a house and a human who liked cats and try to move in. But I was not close to much civilization and I would have to give up my freedom. But that may be better than starving or freezing to death this winter. So I was torn thinking about my options. Options would not put food on my plate, so to speak, though.

Up ahead I saw what looked to be the remains of an old stone fence that someone had built many years ago. I went over to investigate it. The stones were tumbling down, littering the ground, and the closer I inspected it, the more it looked like an old well instead of a fence. Someone had propped up a large piece of plywood in it so that no one could fall into it. The plywood was rotting away and only bugs and snakes could now crawl or slither inside. Suddenly I remembered what Romeo had told me about his bad experience falling into the well years ago. I wondered if this could possibly be the same well that had been near his former home. Surely it couldn't be since Romeo had said that the speculators were buying the old farm house to create a housing development. I decided to explore a bit more.

I saw an opening in the trees that looked like it could be a field and I trotted toward it. At the edge of the woods I scanned the area and saw that it indeed had once been a meadow or a pasture. The field was being overtaken by weeds, but it could have been nice grass at one time, that may have been used to feed a horse. I became a bit excited at the prospect of possibly finding Romeo's old homestead. Swiveling my head I began to head south, toward what looked like a concrete slab. When I reached it, I could tell that this was what was left of someone's home. Walking around the edge, I got the feeling of déjà vu. This really may have been where Romeo was born and was a kitten before he and his mama and sister were taken away. Exploring further, I saw someone, probably a child, had scrawled a name in the concrete. The writing said, "Beauty." There was even a horseshoe print in the old cement near the name. This was it! Beauty was the name of Romeo's horse friend! What a strange coincidence! I wish I could have told Romeo about this discovery, but alas, he had been adopted into a fine home and had probably forgotten all about this place.

But where were all the houses that were supposed to have been built here? Romeo had stated that the farmland was to be turned into a subdivision, but there wasn't a house in sight. Wait! I looked far off into the distance and I could see a few houses that probably constituted a neighborhood. What had happened during the time when the land was purchased and now, when there wasn't anything but a concrete foundation left? Who knew? Maybe the developer had gone bankrupt or had some misfortune come upon him.

I continued to check around and saw what had probably been an old shed in the far corner of the property. The shed had definitely seen better days and it was practically falling in on itself; a strong wind would probably knock it down. The wood was weathered grey and beaten. One side was mostly gone and there were just holes where windows had once been. A creaky door swung on rusty hinges. Cautiously I walked over, my ears perked to catch any hint of danger. Before going inside, I sniffed the air and it smelled mousy. Ah! A fresh mouse for dinner, maybe? That would be satisfying. I decided not to use the door since it looked so precarious, leaning to one side, so I stepped slowly inside where the wall used to be. It was dark inside, even with the one side exposed and my eyes dilated to accommodate the darkness. As I turned the corner, I could not only hear but feel the presence of mice in the old shed. My nose twitched and my whole body zeroed in on the faint scratching along the far wall. I crouched down to make myself less visible and I could feel my tail switching back and forth. All my senses were on full alert. There were still some remains of old straw on the floor and I could picture the shed as it was when Romeo was growing up here as a kitten, playing in the straw. What used to be the stall for Beauty had deteriorated so it was barely recognizable but I knew what it was. My eyes were drawn to the top of the door where a rusty horseshoe was still hanging above it. It was almost like being transported back in time vicariously through the story Romeo had told me. I could picture him and Juliet and their mother living in this place, sharing the space with the horse.

My attention was still riveted on the mouse area. I crept slowly toward the noises and then I spotted them. Not just one but a family of mice! There must have been five or six little gray bodies huddled together in a furry pile. My hunting instinct was high and I was hungry. The two are separate behaviors in cats but many people mistake them for the same. Even a well-fed cat will still hunt small prey including birds, but in much fewer numbers than the bird lovers espouse. If people don't want their cats to kill birds, they need to keep them indoors. Many people think it's cruel to keep cats inside, but actually it is cruel to allow them to go outdoors where many dangers await them including speeding cars, dogs, coyotes, hawks, foxes and sadistic humans.

Anyway, I had to eat to keep up my strength. That night I ate well, slept soundly on the straw which made a comfortable bed, and decided to stay a few days in Romeo's old home. The shed provided a place where I could stay out of the cold and damp weather and I needed to rest.

IVORY'S NEW HOME

Mariana drove slowly toward home while Ivory stayed with her on the front seat. Exhausted, the white cat absorbed some air conditioning from the vent and put her paw on Mariana's leg. This seemed to please Mariana and she petted her while she was driving.

"I don't know where you came from, but you're going home with me. I hope you get along with other cats, since I live with a houseful of them," she told Ivory.

Ivory thought to herself, "Yes, I do like other cats. I'm not very territorial. I just hope the others will like me. Wow! One minute I'm suffering on the hot pavement in the store's parking lot and the next I'm in a cat lady's car! How lucky can I get?"

Ivory regarded her savior driving next to her. The lady had long, dark hair that was pulled back into a ponytail. Ivory guessed that she was middle-aged. She kept her eyes on the road but continued to stroke the cat. Ivory appreciated the soft touch and then she began to purr.

"What a nice cat! How did you possibly wind up in the parking lot? You must have been someone's pet because you don't look too malnourished. I think you could use some good food and some TLC, though."

"Yes, I really could do with some TLC," Ivory thought. "I'd really just like to have a good home and a comfortable life with a caring person. Maybe she is that person."

"I probably should see if you have a microchip and that would tell me if you actually belong to someone."

"Oh no, I don't have one. Don't bother taking me."

"Or maybe we'll see how things work out at my house and you'll become my cat."

"That may be very nice," Ivory reflected.

The car pulled up at a sweet-looking bungalow. It looked sturdily built of brick and sported brick walkways lined with flowers. A few butterfly bushes had attracted a score of brightly-colored winged creatures. There was a front porch with comfortable wicker chairs and a table brightened with flowers in a vase. Ivory saw a big orange and white cat with one eye peering out at the car from a window. The eye was a bit startling to Ivory since she had never seen a one-eyed cat. She wondered if the cat's name was Jack.

"How many cats does this lady have?" she wondered. "Will I fit in with them?"

Mariana put the car in park and reached over to pick up Ivory who didn't complain. The cat clung to her arms as she walked up to the front door. She was glad to be able to escape the heat.

Upon entering the house, Ivory could immediately smell and sense the presence of other felines. It wasn't unpleasant; she instinctively knew she should be wary, however. She continued to hold onto Marian's arm and resisted being put on the floor.

"It's ok. Our little family will welcome you and you don't have to be afraid."

Slowly Ivory let Mariana slide her to the carpet where she was greeted by the one-eyed cat. This was the one who spotted them as they arrived a few minutes ago. Charlie immediately began sniffing the air around Ivory's head and Ivory pulled back, just to be on the safe side. Charlie's fur remained flat on his back which was a good sign.

"Who are you?" he inquired.

"I'm Ivory. Who are you?"

"Charlie. Where did you come from?"

"Wellllll, most recently from the grocery store parking lot."

Charlie looked at her quizzically.

"It's a long story; I'll tell you about it later."

"I'm not surprised. Mariana rescues cats and I'm sure you needed rescuing."

"If you only knew…..Uh, what happened to your eye?"

"Some years ago I started getting cataracts, no pun intended. I couldn't see out of it, so I had an operation to remove it. I'm fine with only one eye. How come you look so scruffy?"

Ivory began to tell him about her experiences at the shelter and her adopter, but just then another cat walked in and immediately spotted her. Little black Cassidy came running over and stopped short of Ivory and arched her back and turned her tail into a bottlebrush.

"Hissss!"

"What? Why are you hissing at me?"

"Grrrrrr!"

Cassidy's eyes narrowed. "Ssssttt!"

"I'm not going to hurt you. Give me a break."

Cassidy growled, "What are you doing here in our house?"

"The nice lady picked me up in a hot parking lot. I almost lost my life in an overheated car. My paws are burned from the pavement. I had a bad experience at the shelter. What else do you want to know?" Ivory asked.

Cassidy considered her answers and said, "I'm not going to like you; I'm black and you're white. Black is beautiful."

"Well, white can be beautiful, too. Who said white and black cats can't get along? The colors exist peacefully on a piano keyboard."

Cassidy began circling Ivory slowly, checking her out from ear tip to tail. "You look a little ratty. What's wrong with you?"

"Oh, I'll tell you about it later. I'm sort of tired now."

Charlie had been watching the exchange from afar and he looked toward the other room to see Lily prance in.

"Did I hear you say you were in a shelter?" she asked Ivory.

Ivory turned to face her and smiled to herself. This was a very pretty cat and a friendly one too.

"Yeah, I spent quite a while there. It took a long time for me to be adopted....I guess it was because I was older and most people wanted kittens. But I felt like the guy who adopted me had bad intentions. My cat intuition told me to get away from him. I don't know exactly why but he sort of gave me the creeps."

Lily told Ivory, "I was in a shelter too before Mariana adopted me. I was very lucky that she picked me."

So, the lady's name was Mariana. Ivory looked around for her and saw she was preparing some cat food for us in the kitchen. She had already carried in the groceries from the car. The white cat was hungry and thirsty. She licked her paws gingerly because they were tender where the steaming asphalt burned them.

Checking out the household furnishings, she saw that there was a cat tree with a few perches close by and a few scratching posts that looked like they had seen better days. Of course, the more beat up a post gets, the better a cat likes it.

"Are you going to live with us?" Lily inquired.

"I don't know. If I get along with you all, maybe so."

"Gggrrrrr!" snarled Cassidy.

"Oh, shut up, Cassidy," said Charlie. "Can't you see that she's hurting?"

"Ok, you cats, come on in and eat," Mariana called.

At the sound of a can being opened, another cat appeared. This one was black and white and was intent on making it to the kitchen before anyone else.

"That's Inbox. He likes to eat. He's good at it." Lily told Ivory.

"Inbox is his name? Does he live on a desk? Are there any other cats here?"

"No, there are just us four."

"How about dogs?"

"No, Mariana is a cat person. I think she likes dogs, but she loves cats."

"That's good to know."

"Let's go eat now."

Ivory didn't need much urging.

Things began to settle down in the next few days. Ivory got to know more about her housemates. Even Cassidy no longer growled or hissed, though she did give Ivory a wide berth. Mariana gave all the cats equal attention and played with them a few times a day. Inbox pretty much stayed on the desk and mainly came down at feeding time. Charlie was not as playful as the others, but he'd sometimes bat at the wand toy or roll a marble across the floor. Ivory and Lily became friends and spent time together in the sunshine. Ivory kept remembering her best friend from the shelter, Kitty, but she knew she would never see her again.

Ivory liked to hear Charlie tease Inbox. He would walk past him when he was lightly snoozing in his favorite place and say, "Hey Inbox! What's on your agenda today? Paying some bills? Filing some papers?"

Inbox would just ignore him.

One day, Mariana walked over to Ivory, stroked her back and said, "Maybe it's about time that we gave you a name."

"But I already have a name that I like," Ivory thought. "Of course, how would Mariana know what it is?" She thought and concentrated on a way to communicate with Mariana. As Ivory went into the kitchen, she looked up at the sink and there it was! A small plastic bottle of Ivory dishwashing soap! Ah ha! The cat jumped up on the counter, something she never had done before and knocked the half-full bottle on the floor. She then jumped down and started batting it around the tiles on the floor. The noise attracted the attention of the other cats and Mariana came into the room and saw Ivory playing with the liquid detergent bottle.

"What are you doing, you silly cat? You have plenty of toys and you know they're scattered all over the house." Mariana bent down to retrieve the bottle and picking it up, she noticed the label. She had never really paid much attention to it before; she had been buying the same brand for years.

"Ivory, original scent, ultra-concentrated. Ivory! The name fits! For an all-white cat, it's perfect!"

"Well, yes it is," Ivory marveled at how fast Mariana picked up on her clue. This was one smart woman. Of course all cat people had a bit more intelligence than the norm.

Mariana studied the cat. "It almost seems like you were trying to tell me that your name was Ivory. Amazing! How smart you are!"

It was mutual admiration on both the cat's and human's parts.

Of course, Cassidy had to make fun of Ivory's name. "Ivory! Elephant's tusk! Piano keys! Ha ha!"

"Oh, leave her alone, Cassidy," Charlie said. "Ivory is a pretty name for a pretty cat."

"Thank you, Charlie. You are very sweet," Ivory purred.

Her fur had started growing back and she was gaining a little weight under the care of Mariana. She was indeed becoming the pretty cat she used to be before her friend Kitty left the shelter. She hoped that Kitty was doing well in her new home and wondered whether she ever thought about her.

MOVING ON

The sadness of Buster's absence was still with me and Monique. It had been weeks since the day Dr. Dean gave Buster the shot. I slept in Buster's bed and his dog scent lingered. Monique quietly packed up the dog dish and the few toys that had not been played with and put them all into a box which went into a closet. Monique did not go out at night as frequently as she used to. She spent most evenings at home, watching TV or reading or emailing her friends on the computer. I stayed close to her at night, trying to make her feel better by purring and rubbing against her ankles. We tried to continue our lives as before, but there was an unspoken emptiness in the house.

Several times I overheard Monique talking to friends on the phone and I caught a few phrases like, "I feel like my life is coming apart." "I don't really want to keep working at the salon for the rest of my life." "I don't know what to do." She was having thoughts of trying to change her lifestyle in a dramatic way and I started to feel uneasy about it. What would she do? Just try to find another job? Still live in this house? And most importantly, keep me with her?

A few times Monique's friend Trina visited and the women chatted over a glass of wine. I had a sixth sense about Trina that made me feel anxious. Trina was pleasant enough, but she didn't seem to be a cat person and I picked up on that by her mannerisms. Sometimes she would glance over at me but didn't really seem to be looking at me, but rather through me. I would retreat to the bedroom on these occasions.

After a few months had passed, Monique came home from work and found me dozing in the sun. She sat down on the floor beside me and stroked my fur as I woke up and stretched. We both looked at each other and I had a strange feeling that something important was about to happen.

"Sweetie, I'm going to be leaving soon. I've enlisted in the military. My job is really a dead end and it's not what I want to do for the rest of my life. I've decided that the best course for me is to join the Air Force while I'm still young enough to make something of my life."

I just stared at Monique for a long minute and looked away. I thought, "How about the best course for MY life? Did you consider that? What will happen to ME? I'm your cat! I'm your cat forever! You and I are supposed to grow old together. No! You can't leave me!" I jumped to my feet and ran to the bedroom and hid underneath the bed. I was betrayed in the worst possible way.

Monique started to cry. The tears fell on the floor as she sat cross-legged and sobbed.

After a while she went into the bedroom and kneeled down to look at me. "I'm so sorry, little one. I feel terrible but this is something I just have to do. Of course you can't come with me, but I've arranged for you to go live with Trina while I'm gone. It will only be for a few years and then I'll come back and get you and we can live together again."

I turned my head away and stared at the wall. I felt like I was going to be sick and I sure was a pitiful sight curled up into a fetal ball. I thought, "This is happening again. Decisions are being made about my life and I don't have any choice. This had been the story of my life ever since I was a little kitten. Why did this always happen to me? Why couldn't she just stay here and try to find another job?" I crammed myself into a corner where the bedpost met the wall and buried my head in my stomach with my tail hiding my face.

Monique started crying again. "Oh what have I done? It's too late now because I've already enlisted and I can't back out because my cat doesn't want me to go."

She craned her neck to see me wrapped up in the far corner. "Jazmine, Trina will give you a good home. She likes cats and plus, it will only be for a few years. Please come out."

I ignored her as only a cat can. I was heartsick over the news and nothing could be done about it. I didn't want to live with Trina. I didn't even like Trina and had the feeling that Trina felt the same way about me. I was just being pawned off on this woman because there was no other place for me to go. I would just become an unwanted cat, living with a person I had no positive feelings for.

Some time went by and I began to feel differently. I gradually changed my mind about Monique leaving and tried to understand her feelings and actions. Monique tried to be extra nice to me, bringing me special treats and spending more time with me. At first I spurned her attentions, but then I figured that I might not ever see her again and she had given me a very good home. She really loved me and I had loved her. She needed to do what she felt was best and if she wasn't happy in her job then she had to change it. I began to allow Monique to pet me again and I slept close to her in her bed. I missed Buster terribly but there was nothing I could do to bring him back. But every time I thought about going to live with Trina I had a bad feeling. I had to do something so that I would not live with Trina, but what? I couldn't really run away. Where would I go?

How would I survive on my own? Was my freedom more important than my comfort? Maybe Trina wasn't so bad after all. I was fluctuating between thinking that I may have a decent home and how much I didn't want this to happen to me.

A month or two passed and my time with Monique was getting short. I became jittery and upset when I thought about my future. Monique began to sell some of her furniture. The chair with the nubby fabric was one of the first pieces to sell and then the couch where I had spent some time lounging. The character of her apartment changed and she started to bring boxes home with her after work. Normally, I would have loved to hide in and sleep in the boxes but now I just didn't have the heart for it. The pictures on the walls came down and were stored in boxes which would be kept in a storage unit for the years Monique would be away. Books were donated to charities and many of Monique's beautiful clothes were also carefully packed. Still, there were some things that remained in place. I began to feel that Monique would be able to put the "pro" in pro-crastinate. Buster's old bed stayed where it had always been. My scratching post stood like a sentinel in the corner. It was as if she was putting off the inevitable by leaving cherished items in their place. But, soon the apartment looked like a bare-bones shadow of itself. The bed remained along with a chair and the table in the dining area. I knew that any day now the movers would come to take away the rest of the furniture and Monique's possessions. Oh, sad day that would be!

Trouble started when I saw the cat carrier on the floor in the living room. This was the day Monique and I were to part ways and I was to go live with Trina. After a good breakfast, Monique tried to put me into the carrier but I refused and ran from her. She looked a bit startled since she and I had always been such good friends and I had always come when she called and done what she wanted.

I hid under the bed and she got down on her knees to peer at me and she said, "Come on, little Jazmine. I hate to do this to you, but you'll have to go in the cat cage so Trina will be able to take you to her house. I'm so sorry. My cat! My beloved cat!" She began to cry. I decided then that I was not going into the cage and I was not going to live with Trina. I stayed under the bed for a few hours while Monique continued to pack her things in the boxes.

A knock at the door scared me and I knew it was the movers who had come to take away everything. I heard some heavy footsteps on the floor and could smell the scent of men who had been perspiring. Boxes were lifted and carried out the door. The table and chairs were now also gone and all that was left was the bed under which I was still hiding and an end table. The two men came into the room and I could see their scuffed shoes and legs on one side.

One man said, "We'll have to dismantle it so it will fit through the door."

Monique told him, "My cat is still under there. Let me see if she'll come out now before you start to take the bed apart."

She again knelt down and looked at me. I looked at her and knew it was my time to go. She reached under the bed but couldn't touch me.

"Please, Jazmine, come out. Please, little one."

I inched away from her.

The mover told her, "She'll come out once we start taking the mattress off."

"Ok, go ahead. I'll catch her if she tries to bolt."

I saw my chance and made a dash out of the bedroom and into the living room. I also saw that the door had been left open and I sprinted toward it. As I paused briefly at the door, I looked back at Monique and gave her a look that said, "I'm so sorry, but I have to live my own life." She ran after me and I shot out the door.

ON MY OWN

I didn't know which way to turn so I just ran down the hallway toward a door. I could hear Monique behind me but I was faster than she was. The door has been propped open for the benefit of the movers and I bolted through it and down the few stairs in a flash.

"Jazmine! Jazmine, come back!" I heard the anguish in Monique's voice as she tried to keep up with me. I continued to run, anywhere, any place, just away from my home or what used to be my home. The sunlight hit me like a bolt of lightning. I hadn't been outdoors in a long time, not since I spent the night in the tree outside my first family's house. I was in the parking lot and there were a few cars in their accustomed spots but I didn't want to scramble under any of them because I knew Monique would then be able to capture me and put me in the cage and take me to Trina's. I spotted some nearby woods and made a beeline, or, for me, a catline for the trees.

"Jazmine!" Monique's voice was getting fainter as she tried to catch her breath and chase me at the same time. "Jazmine…..j a z m i n e….." I turned to look at her one last time and saw she had stopped running but was still watching me as I made my way into the woods.

"Bye bye, Monique," I tried to project my thoughts toward her. "I loved you but it is time for me to go." I flicked my tail and continued on my way, deeper into the woods.

THE COLD WINTER

I looked outside at the low-hanging clouds. They scudded across a steel sky and threatened a bad day at black rock, or, in my case, at the old shed in Romeo's former yard. Light snow began to fall, soon covering the ground with a light blanket of white. I shivered and fluffed my fur to try to stay warm. I crept back into the corner where the straw helped to keep me from freezing the night before and curled up into a tight circle with my tail over my nose. Uggh. I didn't like to be cold and this winter had promised to be a record-setter for low temperatures. The acorns that had fallen a few months ago were huge and covered the ground in heaps under the oaks. The wooly worms were indeed wooly with their brown and black sections constantly on the move. The summer critters were either hibernating, had migrated southward, or were dead. No colorful butterflies flitted around the wildflowers, the bees were nowhere to be seen, and the other insects had disappeared. This was somewhat good news for me, as the fleas that had so irritated me were also gone. Oh, how I hated those blood-suckers! Nasty little disease-carrying pests they were. I missed the warmth of the sun, kissing my fur as I lounged lazily in a ray. I hadn't seen the sun in many days and when it did briefly appear, it was weak like tasteless tea and not the comforting sun of summer.

Besides the woes of the unforgiving winter, I was becoming lonely. There were no other cats around, or even any dogs. I remembered Buster, my dog buddy, and I wished he was still here to provide a black pillow for me to lay my head. I missed him so much it was painful to even think about him. My other cat friends were probably living lives of contentment in their adoptive homes by now. I wished them well and then thought of my best friend, Ivory. I wondered what had happened to her and hoped she was secure and cozy in someone's home. Maybe she had a warm lap on which to snooze. She well deserved it. A picture of Monique crossed my mind and I hoped things were progressing career-wise for her now that she was in the Air Force. I pondered my decision again for the hundredth time. Should I have stayed and gone to live with Trina? I knew she really didn't want me and I didn't want to live with her. Was my choice the right one? During the warm months, I felt like it was, but now when times were tough, I questioned my judgment. Weary of these thoughts, I drifted off into a catnap as the snow continued to insulate and pad the earth outside.

I was awakened sometime later by a tickling on my back. I realized that something was crawling on me! I jumped up and shook myself and turned around to see what it was and found a spider on my fur! I hate spiders! I scratched it off with my hind foot and watched it quickly scurry across the floor of the shed and hide itself in a far corner. I get goose bumps whenever I even see one and I would never think of eating one. Some cats like to play with them, but the thought of touching one creeped me out. By this time I was wide awake, thinking about how there may be brothers, sisters, aunts, uncles, and children of the spider just lying in wait until my guard was down to pounce on me. I began to lick my fur and gave myself a good bath. Then I remembered the snow and looked out a hole where a window had been. It was deep! Probably about a foot deep and it covered everything. The white stuff was still falling, but this time in huge flakes. It was still overcast and dark and now it was getting colder. I was stuck in the shed because the snow was deeper than I was tall. Even worse, I was stuck in the shed with an army of spiders. Oh, double uggh! I spent the remainder of the night in a semi-wakeful state, constantly checking my surroundings for more creepy crawlers.

The light awakened me in the morning. It was a very bright, even blinding light that sprang through the window holes at me. Was I in heaven? No, that couldn't be right because it was too cold. It was terribly cold and I buried my head in my stomach and curled my tail over my nose to keep it warm. Even my bones were cold. But I couldn't go back to sleep so I decided to get up, and stretched to help limber up my body. I peeked through one of the holes and regarded a magical scene. Everything was covered with snow. The trees, weeds, the concrete slab where the house used to be, the fields and as far as I could see, snow had obliterated it all. As my eyes grew accustomed to the bright, I noticed that there were diamonds sparkling everywhere! The cold sunshine glittered on the scene, making it an other-worldly place. The sky was as blue as a clean swimming pool and the frozen earth enchanted me. Nothing was moving outside. There were no birds or any creatures stirring, not even a mouse. A mouse! Now my hunger pangs kicked in and I remembered the mouse nest in the corner. I caught a whiff of them and slowly crept over to the area where they were rustling about. I spotted a small gray one, and before it knew what was what, I had devoured my breakfast. I could have used some water to quench my thirst, but none was available in the shed. I would have to make do later with some snowmelt.

Deciding to explore a bit further, I went over to where the fresh snow had drifted in and put my paw in it. I withdrew it quickly and licked it. I was shed-bound and I knew not how long I would be stranded in Romeo's shed. If the temperatures didn't warm up for a while, the snow would hinder my movement outside. I was not a mole that could tunnel my way out and I wasn't too fond of the snow either. I had some experience with snow in a past winter but I had never seen it this deep. I did admit that it was beautiful, though.

The rustling of the mice continued. I thought they must be having their own breakfast. And so it goes, the chain of life. I didn't feel bad about having to eat some of them. Besides, they multiplied so quickly, there would soon be more to take the place of the eaten ones.

I needed to relieve myself and of course there were no litter boxes in the shed. I would have to make my own in another corner, far away from where the spider had disappeared. As I was attending to the business at hand, I happened to glance up at the wood rafters and saw two beady little black eyes staring at me. This was startling and I slowly backed away toward my sleeping corner. What could that possibly be? Not being used to outdoor wild animals, I had to always be aware of my surroundings and whatever this was looking down on me had made me realize that I couldn't slack off in my defense. The eyes followed me and made me uncomfortable. With my back to the wall, I hunkered down and watched the unblinking eyes that swiveled to watch my movements. Well, at least I hadn't been attacked; I was just the object of scrutiny. I decided to wait it out. The dazzling sun moved slowly around the sky and I could tell that it soon would be close to noon. The eyes closed and I figured this was a nocturnal animal since it had not shown itself yet. That made me more uneasy because even though I was nocturnal, I also liked to snooze at night.

So, as I now counted, there were four different species inhabiting the shed: the mice, the spiders, the unknown creature on the rafter and me. There may be more that I didn't know about. I wasn't actually inhabiting the shed; I was merely passing some time before the snow melted so I could continue on my way. I turned around several times in my corner on the straw and made myself cozy. I dozed off and on, dreaming about my dear friend Ivory who I wouldn't see again and my departed buddy, Buster.

I woke up to a scrabbling noise from above and saw a figure scootching down a beam close to my bed. The blinding light had faded and it was now dusk. I knew the night animals would soon become active and I would need to be on my guard. Right now, I watched the creature as it clumsily made its way toward the floor. I crouched in my straw and smelled an unusual odor. This was something I had not encountered yet and I could feel the fur begin to rise on my back. My ears went flat on my head for protection in case this was an unfriendly animal. Plunk! It plopped down and gathered its wits before putting its nose to the ground, sniffing my scent. I could see the ugly gray fur and fat body and what looked like a rat's tail swishing behind it. This must be a possum! I didn't have experience with possums but this one was encroaching on my territory and I didn't like that. Not at all. I hissed at it which stopped the fat one from coming closer. Fixing me with a glower, it hissed back. I emitted a low growl and put my body on high alert. My fur stood on end and my hackles were raised. This possum was larger than I was but maybe I could frighten it away using my wits. I decided that possums were creatures uglier than rats on drugs. I also hoped that its family wasn't living in the shed. Another thing that made me uneasy was the fact that the possum was backing me into a corner, cutting off my escape route. It also had a funky smell, like a moldy old sock. Nasty! My sensitive nose twitched and I tried to deflect the odor by breathing in a shallow manner but the creature still reeked.

"Ssssstt!"

I responded with a snarl and a hiss. How unpleasant this was! Surely I wouldn't have to leave the barn and venture out into the snow because of this creature. Then I heard little scrabbles from the corner where I had made my toilet and saw the possum turn to peer at the dim, dark area on the other side of the barn.

The possum turned with its snout to the ground and shuffled off to investigate the noises. Maybe I was saved after all and could get some rest. My senses would have to be on high alert though. I surely didn't want those sharp yellow teeth anywhere near my body.

I dreamed vividly about Buster that night. I saw him romping on a warm beach and running through the waves having a great time. His black fur was thick and shined in the sunlight. I tried to call out to him and for a moment I thought he actually looked my way and grinned, in that way some dogs have. I felt comforted that his spirit was still alive and that he was whole again. I awoke and it was still dark but there were no other sounds coming from the spider, possum, or mice corners.

The next few days were spent mostly waiting for it to warm up enough for the snow to melt. I wanted to leave this place, even though there was a steady supply of food. Several times I had the impression that I was being watched and I was sure the possum had its eye on me. I also had a feeling that there would be some hostilities before I could make my exit.

The winter had long worn out its welcome. It was cold in the shed and that didn't make me happy. The nights were the worst when I had to be semi-awake, watching out for the animals that were out to get me. One night in another dream, I was in my former home, curled up next to Monique, with Buster on the floor close to her feet. There was soft music coming from the TV and she was reading a book. My head was resting on her lap and she would gently stroke my fur while I purred a melody for both my friends. Then I awoke, realizing those days were over, never to be relived again. If cats could cry, I would have at that moment. My life was a difficult one now, and there were few pleasures or comforts to be had. What had I been thinking when I ran away? At least Trina would have provided me with food and shelter. I had wanted to be my own cat, doing what I wanted to do without having someone else make decisions that would chart the course of my life. What life was this, where I was freezing in an old run-down shed that I had to share with spiders and possums? I was depressed.

Gradually the weather warmed a bit so I could see the snowmelt beginning to drip off what was left of the roof. I stretched and ventured out of my corner to check out the white outdoors. There was a shallow area where the snow had formed a water hole as such. I stepped out on the mud and went over to drink some of the cold liquid. It was rather refreshing and I was thankful it was so close to the shed. Periodically small sheets of ice dropped from the trees to become crystal daggers in the snow beneath. I took note of that and determined that I would have to stay away from the undersides of the tree branches so I wouldn't be speared. Maybe another night or two spent in the shed would be sufficient and then I could continue on my journey, wherever it would lead me.

That night I wasn't so fortunate. The warmth had helped to awaken the creatures in the shed. At first I saw a large spider coming straight toward me. This one seemed to have at least 12 legs and it looked ravenous. Was it a tarantula? A black widow? A brown recluse? My heart began to beat faster and I looked for an escape route. The eyes practically glowed in the gloom of the old shed. If I knew some curse words, I would have used them, but I wasn't in the habit of cussing. I sprang up and sidled around the spider, keeping a close watch on it. The creepy one crawled into my bed and that alarmed me. Now, where was I going to sleep? All the corners were taken and I couldn't go back to my little area. From the right, I heard the possum moving around in the straw. I could feel the piercing stare fixed on my body like it was a bulls eye. I might as well have a target tattooed on my side. If so, it would have been a "cattoo." I was in no mood for joviality so I didn't even think my little pun was humorous. I didn't want to get too close to the large opening because it was very cold there with the winter wind whistling through. I was fairly miserable. I tried to scratch out a bit of straw to construct a makeshift bed but it was inadequate so I just lay down on the dirt.

Sometime in the night I heard and smelled a skunk outside. Oh great, just what I needed. The odor was piercing and my sensitive nose wrinkled in disgust. Hopefully this obnoxious creature wouldn't come into the shed. What else could go wrong this bleak night? I kept my vigil for a while and then I saw its pointy snout snuffling around what was left of the side wall. My eyes watched the black and white one warily. It shuffled back and forth and seemed to be looking for something. Maybe searching for a little cat for its dinner? I sighed a small cat sigh. The skunk finally spied me trying to hide in the sparse straw. It sauntered toward me and then I saw the tail point skyward! Again, if I knew how to cuss, this would have been the appropriate time. I jumped up and clumsily climbed the pole up toward the possum area. Better a possum bite than a skunk spraying. I landed on a rafter above the skunk and prayed that it didn't know how to climb the old pole. I was spared this time because instead of being sprayed with the worst-smelling skunk stench, I was above looking down on this intruder. After a few minutes I saw the beast exit through the opening. But just then, I heard a low hissing coming from another rafter behind me. I edged around to confront the possum. The fat brute bared its ugly teeth and I screamed. All my frustrations seemed to be expelled in that one loud, extended scream. The animal seemed determined to get rid of me and I frantically looked around for a way to escape. As my stomach contracted in small spasms of fright, I knew I would have to jump down to get away. So I did. I landed on all fours and headed out the opening into the cold white night. I was leaving Romeo's former home where he had been so content and I had been so unhappy.

CITY KITTY

The remainder of the winter was spent scrounging around trying to stay alive and constantly on the move. I would sleep anywhere there was a bit of shelter...in a branch of a tree, near the base of a tree's trunk, and once even in an old abandoned car. The car must have been junked many years ago because it was overgrown with weeds that had died in the freezing weather and a small tree was growing up inside where the back seat used to be. This decomposing hulk had at one time been painted a two tone green color. The metal corroded silver logo was still affixed to the back of the trunk and spelled "Ponti", which I was sure meant "Pontiac." I spent several days and nights close to the car. The seats had disintegrated and the metal parts were rusting away but the car's skeleton provided a little protection from predators and the terrible winter. I wondered who had owned and driven such a car and why it had wound up in the woods. Maybe someone had stolen it long ago and wanted to hide it. But I could tell it had been built like a tank and probably had many stories to tell if it could talk.

I hunted early in the dawn hours and before it became dark each day. There was not much to eat and I was losing some weight. I kept hoping that warmer weather would soon spring forth.

Again I was changing my zip code and one day found myself out of the woods and in a more populated area. The trees and leaf litter gave way to peoples' yards and civilization. I had sensed that my travels were bringing me toward human habitation and I was ambivalent about that but thought I could handle it since I am not afraid of people. However, I stayed hidden during the days because I felt that I had to be cautious in dealing with humans who might want to interfere with my way of life again. I did not want to go back to living in a cage, or living with Trina or living with a family that did not want me. Now, I had to be aware not so much of possums or coyotes or skunks, but of pet dogs. It seemed they could smell me miles away and then they began a chorus of harsh barks and loud warning howls. Being a cat, I did not smell because I keep myself immaculately clean, but they still picked up the clues that I was in the neighborhood. For the most part, they stayed in their own yards behind protective underground fences or in outdoor enclosures. Sometimes, though, I had to climb a tree to avoid a dog that was allowed to run amok through the community. Why don't people keep their dogs in their own yards? Dogs can cause so much havoc when they are running loose without supervision. One advantage of my being close to peoples' houses was that I found a few more shelters to sleep in such as open garages or backyard outbuildings. I had to be careful that I was not locked up inadvertently when taking advantage of a warmer place to spend a few hours.

I even found some suitable food available that wasn't still breathing when I devoured it. A few people kept their cats outdoors and left food on the doorsteps for them. Trying to avoid the resident cats, I would eat quickly and scamper off to find a quiet place. I didn't know if the cats would be friendly or hostile and I didn't want to get into any fights. I didn't feel bad about stealing this food because I was sure the owners had an endless supply of cat food for their cat companions in their houses.

One new phenomenon I had to contend with was people's vehicles. I did not have much experience with them except the few times I had ridden inside them. Just seeing how fast they sped by me sent shivers up my spine. I vowed that I would not become a cat pancake on the pavement so I kept away from busy roads and streets where the speeding cars and trucks were. They still scared me though, and the loud noises emanating from the engines and occasional honks from the horns were enough to instill a healthy respect for them.

I was traveling slower through the suburbs as I was savoring some decent cat food occasionally. I was also glad that the days were beginning to get warmer and the nights weren't so cold. I was beginning to think I might survive after all I had been through lately. My disposition improved every day I could lie in the sun and absorb the rays. I actually felt happy about my situation and thought it really was a wonderful life. I was free. Free to do whatever I wanted and no one to direct any events that would impact my life. But I still felt I was missing an important aspect. I could not enjoy the warmth and close contact of a human's lap. I wanted to sleep on a soft bed. Monique had indeed spoiled me and pampered me during the time I was with her. She was the ideal pet mom and had given me everything I wanted. I could still smell the delightful aroma of the fresh catnip drying in the microwave that long-ago day. Heaven on earth! How fortunate I had been to live with her and Buster. So many cats will never have it so good. But this was my choice, what I had chosen to do. That night I curled up under someone's porch and could hear the sound of a TV inside the house. I dreamed of better days.

The next day dawned clear and warmer. Spring was here and I was again on the move. I traveled closer into what I believed was a city. As the day progressed I avoided more and more cars and stayed close to the buildings lining the boulevards. A few stores were opening and people started passing me on the street. A few glanced my way, but most were in a hurry to get to work or wherever they were going. I didn't know where I was going but was just walking and hoping to find a decent breakfast.

The storefronts were decked out in pastel colors, especially those that sold clothing. I knew the owners were looking forward to selling clothes that reflected the spring season. Then, I had a strange feeling that I was being watched and stopped on the sidewalk. As I looked around, I happened to look up at what was a multi-story apartment building. There was a door-man on the ground level standing ready to open and close the door under an elaborate awning. Clothed in what looked like an upscale band member's uniform, complete with gold epaulets, he smiled at the residents who entered or exited. He didn't notice me but I was still getting some vibes from the building. This was weird. I heard a sound coming from up above, around the third floor, like a scraping on a chalkboard or on a windowpane. It was like someone's claws were beckoning to me through a window in the building. I squinted and looked more closely at the window. It was a cat, clawing and scratching a window. What the heck? The cat then rubbed against the glass and looked straight at me. Those large eyes looked so familiar. I then noticed the cat's body had no fur and was wrinkled like Scorpio's, the cat who I had befriended at the shelter. The cat blinked and seemed to almost wink at me. I kept staring up at him. Was that Scorpio, the privileged cat whose people had left him at the shelter when they moved to Italy? Surely it couldn't be. This was too much of a coincidence. But were some things coincidences or did they just seem to be? The cat raised his paw to the window like he was waving at me. I raised my paw at him. He immediately got up and arched his back and then stood on his hind legs with both front paws on the window. Wow! This really was Scorpio! He was beckoning me to come in! I really couldn't believe I was seeing my friend again, living here in the city.

I decided to try to get into the apartment building and turned toward the doorman who was busy letting people in and out through the door. Maybe he would let me in, too. I went over and started to walk through the door when he stuck his foot out in my path, blocking my way. How rude! I tried to jump over his foot and he caught me under my stomach and sort of kicked me back out onto the sidewalk. Marching band man was obviously not a cat person. I didn't like being kicked and I thought I could sneak in some other way, but he seemed to be a permanent fixture in the doorway and was not going to allow me access. I went back out where I could look up at Scorpio. He was still in the window, looking down at me. I shrugged my shoulders and I knew he could understand what the problem was. I was going to have to communicate with him from three floors down. I parked myself on the sidewalk, situated so that I could see Scorpio, but out of the way of the pedestrians' feet. We watched each other for quite a while and presently a lady from the building came out the door and put a pie plate in front of me with some dry cat food in it. I was very hungry and gobbled it quickly. She stayed close by and when I was finished, I rubbed her ankles in appreciation. She reached down to pet me and I gave her a look of gratitude. Thank goodness for kind people. The lady then picked up the tin and disappeared into the building.

All the time Scorpio had been observing what was happening. He sort of danced around in the window and I blinked my eyes a few times, signaling him that I was ok. I remembered how depressed he had been at the shelter because he thought no one would adopt him because he was so unusual-looking. When we were there, many people would see Scorpio and remark on his looks. Some of the comments weren't very nice and that would make Scorpio feel sad. The children especially would point at him and a few said he looked like an old rat, which was very insensitive. I assume they thought he couldn't understand what they were saying about him. Without realizing it, so many people were being unkind to poor Scorpio. But now I could see that someone did adopt him and it looked like he had a very comfortable existence. So I figured that there was a cat for everyone who wanted one. It would be boring if everyone wanted the same type of cat.

I spent the day on the sidewalk. A few people would stop and talk to me and stroke my back. Then they hurried off to attend to their own lives. Most of the people didn't take much notice of me and that was okay. I really wanted to go upstairs to see Scorpio but that wasn't going to happen with the doorman on duty.

As the afternoon slipped into dusk, a new doorman appeared, wearing the same type of uniform. I hoped this new one was more lenient than the day shift one. Workers started arriving home from their jobs and the doorman opened and shut the door for them. I walked over and tried to look pretty. The doorman ignored me until I attempted again to gain entrance. This man sort of snarled at me and looked like he was going to really kick me to hurt me, so I figured I should back off. Looking up I could see Scorpio relaxing in the window. He looked contented and satisfied and I was happy for him.

As I was watching him, a man appeared behind him. Scorpio looked up and the man picked up the cat. Scorpio nuzzled him and wrapped his paws around the man's neck. The man gently caressed his cat companion. They stood there like that for a few minutes until he put Scorpio down on the windowsill. My friend looked at me long and hard and I knew it was his dinnertime and he would have to go. He raised his paw in farewell and I arched my back and smiled at him. We didn't need words to convey our feelings. How wonderful it was that my old friend now had a good life and a person to care for him.

THE FISH TRUCK

I left Scorpio's apartment building as soon as it was dark. I didn't know where I would spend the night, but I was hoping for a safe place, away from all the commotion of the city streets. I wasn't that hungry since the nice lady had fed me earlier. The hustling city didn't appeal to me that much because I didn't really feel secure wherever I went. But at least there were no possums or skunks to cope with. I stayed away from the curbs and tires of the parked cars. I shadowed close to the edge of the buildings and store fronts. The air cooled down but wasn't as cold now that spring was near. A few people came out to walk their dogs, but thank goodness they were all on leashes (the dogs, not the people.) Some would bark at me and a few tried to leap at me, but I sidestepped them and hurried away. I investigated some side streets and could smell the aromas drifting outside from a few restaurants. The delicious smell of seafood was enticing. I even saw some dumpsters behind these establishments that looked promising, but then I decided that I was too proud to scramble into any of them. Besides, there might be rats or even worse, spiders inside.

I stayed at a steady pace and continued on my way. I guessed it was about 11:00 p.m. and my legs were getting tired so I kept looking for a place to sleep but didn't see anything suitable. Back on the main boulevard, I saw a large delivery truck parked next to the curb. The lettering on the side read, "Coastal Seafood" and the back cargo door was up. No one was nearby and again, I could sniff the odor of fresh fish and other shellfish wafting out to tempt my senses. Glancing around, I decided to chance it and leaped into the back of the truck. The darkened cavern was crammed with shipping boxes which I assumed were packed with seafood of all sorts. It was cold in there to keep the fish frozen. I cautiously made my way down a narrow aisle to the back and began to claw at a box, hoping to tear it open and take advantage of some raw fish. Yes, a sushi dinner really appealed to me. I had torn open a side of the box and stuck my paw into it when all of a sudden I heard a loud bang and knew that I was in trouble. The cargo door had slammed shut or had been closed by someone and I was trapped! How ironic that I was trapped in a seafood delivery truck. Forgetting my sushi, I began to panic and ran around the inside of the truck, looking for an escape route. There were none and it was now pitch dark inside. Seafood smells aside, I experienced a sense of confined dismay. Alarmed at my predicament, I didn't know what to do. The truck started moving and I was frightened at the prospect of the unknown. Where was the driver going? What was I to do? I felt control of my life slipping away and I hated that feeling. Who knew how long I would be inside this rolling fish transport? Maybe we would only go a few blocks and I would be free again. Or maybe not. I hunkered down among the boxes and could feel my heart beating too fast. Oh why hadn't I been more careful?

The driver kept going, stopping at lights and continuing on his way. I could barely hear the sound of a few horns honking and then the sounds ceased. The stops at lights became fewer and I figured that we were headed out of the city. I liked adventure, but not this kind where I was unaware of my destination. My paw pads were cold on the steel floor and I jumped up on a box that had skidded off the top of a group of boxes. The driver picked up some speed and I clung to the box.

"Let meeoowwt!" I cried out, to no avail, of course. The driver couldn't hear me for the noise of the engine and I dreaded to think about what he would have done if he discovered a cat in amongst the frozen fish. I was also hoping that I wouldn't be frozen like the fish because it seemed to be getting colder by the minute.

Of course, I knew it was my fault for allowing myself a bit of indulgence when I should have kept my paws on the pavement and found a cozy place to spend the night in the city. I could have gone back to Scorpio's building and watched him through his window as he luxuriated in his owner's apartment. But not now.

I didn't know exactly how long I had been in the back of the truck but guessed it was about a half hour's drive from the city. I was now shivering in the cold and hoping the truck would stop so I could escape. It was really cold. The temperature must have been below freezing to keep all the fish fresh and prevent thawing. I hoped that this wasn't a long-distance truck ride to some place far away. I would definitely be a frozen cat by then. I could feel the truck lumbering along and the cooler vibrating above my head. The fish smell was starting to nauseate me too. I wondered how fresh these fish actually were. All sorts of strange thoughts about fish began to fill my mind. These must have been caught on the coast and immediately frozen aboard boats before being loaded on the distribution trucks to then be delivered to various restaurants. How had those fish felt when they were caught and iced down? Do fish have the same feelings that cats do? Does it hurt when a hook pierces their mouthparts? I understood how they fight and try to escape when a human hooks them. I thought about all the cans of fish-flavored cat food I had consumed at Monique's house. Even some of the dry food had fishy ingredients added to it, maybe bones, scales and innards for all I knew. My opinion of fish as a food source began to change as I rode along in the arctic depths of the truck. I thought that I would stick to mice and the occasional bird after this. And one more thought...why don't the cat food manufacturers make mice-flavored food? Would that be against FDA regulations? Was I beginning to hallucinate?

I curled up tightly to conserve my body heat and wrapped my tail over my nose to keep it from freezing. I was really uncomfortable, clinging to the fish box and being jostled around when the truck turned corners. I was disoriented and couldn't think about where I would end up. My ears were exposed to the cold and I hoped frostbite wouldn't set in and they would have to be amputated. Would I ever get a break?

"Let meeeooowwwttt!" I whimpered. My voice was getting weaker. Finally I could feel the truck slowing down and I hoped it would come to a stop so I could have a chance to escape. The truck did stop and I heard the driver get out and the door slam behind him. I knew we weren't in the city but where were we? Would I have a chance to get out of this ice box? I stretched my muscles and crept close to the back panel in case it was lifted. I didn't want the driver to see me, but then again, if he did, so what? I could run faster than he could and he wouldn't be interested in chasing me anyway.

After an interminably long and cold time, I could faintly hear the driver's footsteps coming closer. Please, PLEASE open the door I prayed. And then I heard the magic sound of the metal cranking up to admit a faint light which temporarily startled me as my eyes adjusted to it. The driver was staring at me! I stared at him. He was face to face with me. I knew my eyes were shining in the darkness like miniature flashlights and I thought it might have scared him since he didn't expect to see a cat in his truck. I gathered my wits and sprang out of the truck, landing on the street, close to the man. He jumped back and muttered a word I won't repeat. He shouted at me, but I was heading out and running for my life. The night air was cool but not as cold as the inside of the truck and it sure felt good to be able to stretch my limbs and be free. Free! I was free again. They say that freedom is not free, but this time, for me, it was. I ran and ran, leaving the fish truck behind until it became a small white box in my rear view mirror.

A NEW BEGINNING

Where was I? All I knew was that I was running down a road with a few buildings on either side, but not as crowded as the city had been. Some cars were parked on both sides and since there was no moving traffic, I just stayed in the middle of the road. I don't know how long I kept up the pace, but after a while I started slowing down to catch my breath. Nothing scared me and everything seemed quiet and peaceful. I moved to the sidewalk and continued walking in the same direction. I needed to find a secure place to sleep and then I saw what I was looking for. In an alley just off the main street, someone had piled up some empty boxes that had apparently been thrown out for the trash. I examined them and decided one would suit my purposes. It didn't smell of fish or anything offensive; it had probably contained computer printer paper. So I turned around a few times and made my "nest" facing the street. I was really exhausted so I dropped off to sleep shortly.

I was awakened early by the noise of a garbage truck banging down the street. The rumble and vibration and the flashing lights of the truck jarred me awake. I knew I had to get out of the box and be on my way. I surely didn't want to be stuck inside a truck again, especially one filled with yucky, smelly garbage where I could be squished. The fish truck had been bad enough.

I bounded out of my sleeping place and took a quick look around. It was still fairly dark, but I could see the sky brightening somewhat in the east. It was chilly, but not too uncomfortable. The main street was still and I didn't see anyone around except for the man operating the trash truck. I turned the opposite way and walked down the sidewalk, sniffing some objects as I went on my way. No cat smells to be found, but a dog pile had been left to decompose close to the curb. Strange how dogs would just "go" anywhere, while cats were very fastidious about their toilet habits.

The town seemed to be very clean with no trash littering the street. Some of the businesses had daffodils and other spring flowers which were just now beginning to bloom in the wooden planters on the sidewalks. It was still too early for the shops to open and I didn't see any people out yet. I really enjoyed this time of day, when the world seemed fresh and clean without the hubris of the day-to-day activities. It was also my hunting time. Time to start looking for today's blue plate special. What would I find here in this town to satisfy my hunger? I was definitely not in the mood for any fishy-type product. Just the memory of the dark, cold and pungent fish smell of the delivery truck turned my stomach. I was counting my blessings that the ride in the truck hadn't been lengthier; I might not be here to explore this new territory if I had remained confined much longer.

I didn't know what day it was, but I was very aware of the signs of early springtime. Someone had left a watering can beside a flower pot and it was full of water. I sniffed the liquid and it seemed ok so I drank my fill of it. The snow had just about melted except for a few accumulations up against the north side of some buildings. I wasn't unhappy to see it go, but knew it was possible to have a freak snowstorm in the unpredictable spring months.

I was leisurely walking down the street observing what I could when I saw a white tail twitching from behind one of the planters. I stopped in my tracks to watch. This was a cat's tail and the end of it moved rapidly back and forth like a teacher wagging a finger at a naughty student. It was pure white and I wanted to see what it was attached to because it briefly reminded me of Ivory, my beautiful friend. It had been quite a while since I had seen her and I longed to be with her again.

I had no idea what had happened to her once I left the shelter.

I was fascinated by the movement and inched a little closer. I saw the rest of the tail that was also white, as white as the recently departed snowstorm. The haunches of this cat were also white. Could this be Ivory? How would she have come to be out here on the street with her back half wiggling as if to pounce on some prey? Surely that would have been too much of a coincidence. My heart started beating faster with a faint hope of recognizing Ivory.

I whispered, "Ivory, is that you?"

Startled, the cat turned around and glared at me.

"You've interrupted my potential breakfast!" the cat exclaimed. I could hear scurrying as the potential breakfast made a getaway.

I looked closely at this white phenomenon in front of me and saw the black splotch of fur on the forehead and realized this cat was not Ivory but was one very upset cat.

"Oh, I'm sorry! I thought you were a friend of mine," I apologized. "I didn't mean to make you mad."

"Well, now I have to go find something else to eat because of you."

My emotions were hard to disguise and I just sat and looked down at the ground. The cat faced me and tentatively sniffed my face. I recoiled a bit but didn't feel threatened. I had to admit that this was a pretty cat and could have been distantly related to Ivory. The cat's coat shimmered white except for the quarter-sized black mark on the face. This was a hefty-sized feline, with muscles that rippled, telling me that he was toned in the muscle department.

"My name is Jazmine. What's yours?"

"Someone named me Mr. Whiskers a few years ago," he informed me.

"Do you have a nickname? Whisk? Mistery?"

"No one calls me anything now because I don't live with anyone."

"That's something we have in common. I don't live anywhere either." The words sounded sad and I felt a pang of homesickness, something I hadn't experienced much before. Briefly I thought of my good fortune having lived with Monique and Buster. But that was in the past.

"What are you doing here? I haven't seen you around," he asked.

I explained how I arrived in town and what I'd been doing since last night. The look on Mr. Whiskers face was unbelieving as if I had made up a fish story.

"You were locked in a fish delivery truck and escaped when the door opened? You were lucky you didn't freeze to death."

"Yes, I know."

Mr. Whiskers just shook his head.

I asked him, "Where do you stay?"

"Oh here and there. Wherever I can find a good source of food. I stay mainly in the town because that's where I'm comfortable. There aren't too many other animals who bother me, except for Flash, who doesn't like anyone."

"Flash? Is that a cat or a dog?"

"He's an unneutered tomcat who hangs around the same places I do. He has a perpetual attitude and is always looking for a fight."

I shivered. "What does Flash look like?" I wanted to be prepared to stay away from this cat who was so unpleasant.

"He is large and strong. He has a dark tabby coat with typical markings of gray and black. He has a big head as many males have when they aren't neutered. He is powerful and you should avoid him if you can."

"Uh oh. Why do they call him 'Flash'?"

"Because he appears suddenly, in a flash. He can sneak up on you and you won't know it until he grabs you by the throat."

I shuddered and asked, "Does Flash live around here?" I was hoping that the answer would be no.

"Yes! He is everywhere you don't want him to be. I got into a fight with him about a year ago and I still have a few scars to prove it."

"Mmmm. I'll be on the lookout for him." I knew Flash was bad news and I thought it may be safer for me to be on my way, wherever that was.

Mr. Whiskers said, "Why don't we look for some breakfast? We could try the cat lady up the street who sometimes feeds us strays."

"Ok I'll go with you," I told him and started tagging along behind him.

We started in the direction of where Mr. Whiskers indicated the cat lady put out food. The streets were becoming busier now that it was getting lighter. We stayed close to the buildings so people wouldn't step on us. A few men rode bicycles in the road on their way to work. The shopkeepers were busy opening their places of business, some sweeping the sidewalk, some tidying up inside the stores. Blinds were opened to admit the sunlight. A few houses were interspersed among the stores and we could tell the inhabitants were awakening to the new day. We could smell some bacon cooking, which appealed to both of us and some coffee that was brewing which didn't. The aromas wafted out of the houses and piqued our senses. The town seemed clean and well-kept. The houses were older, possibly built in the early part of the 20th century with small, neat yards, many bursting with color from the spring flowers. We weren't in a big hurry and I had a chance to look around to examine the surroundings. This might not be a bad place to spend some time, providing food was available and I could avoid Flash. I tried not to think of him.

After a few blocks, Mr. Whiskers pointed out the cat lady's house. It was a two-story clapboard with a wrap-around porch and some wicker chairs and a table. I could see a bowl of water on the porch and I was anxious to quench my thirst, so I climbed the stairs and gently lapped up some of the liquid. It was then I had the feeling I was being watched and jerked my head up and swiveled it to the left to see two cats at the far end of the porch watching me. Not knowing what to expect, I narrowed my eyes and crouched down near the water dish.

Mr. Whiskers said, "Don't be afraid; those are just some of the other strays the cat lady feeds. Many of us hang around here because it is easy to eat some good food without too many hassles. Some of the cats even sleep on the porch when the weather permits."

I could hear some noises in the house and was hoping that the cat lady would bring out the food soon. The two cats on the porch moved in a little closer and I could see that they were probably related to each other. They were both orange tabbies with white paws and white streaks on their foreheads. They didn't look like they would be threatening so I just stayed put and waited.

Presently I heard the door unlock and we all turned toward it to see a little old lady step out on the porch. She was wearing a blue sweat suit and her curly gray hair framed a compassionate-looking face.

She looked kindly at us and gazed closely at me said, "Why, you're new! I haven't seen you here at all.

You must be hungry. I wonder how all these cats find me….there must be a feline network that only cats know about. Well, it doesn't matter; I'm glad you came and you're welcome to stay as long as you want. And good morning to the rest of you."

The cats edged closer and the two orange tabbies rubbed up against the lady's legs. I then saw two more cats jump up on the porch. This was a regular kitty haven, it seemed. These cats were older and a bit on the chubby side. Both of them were tuxedo cats with beautiful contrasting black and white markings. They eyed me and then ignored me. We all expectantly waited as the lady put down dishes of dry and canned food. Each cat had his or her own dish; we weren't required to eat out of someone else's dish, which I appreciated.

The lady then sat down in one of the rocking chairs and watched us as we consumed our breakfast. She smiled as she rocked and I felt comfortable.

All of a sudden, a big cat appeared from the side of the house. He whizzed by me and crowded out one of the tuxedos to gobble up what was left of the food.

"Ggrrrr!" snarled the tuxedo.

"SSSssss!" growled one of the orange and whites.

"Hisssss!" said Mr. Whiskers as he backed into the wall.

"Cats! Cats!" cried the cat lady. "Let's let Flash eat too."

Oh! So this was Flash! He was just as Mr. Whiskers had described him: big and powerful with a large head and a huge cattitude. He grumbled under his breath as he inhaled the food.

"Let's not have any trouble on this fine morning, ok?" the lady implored us. I could see the other cats' tails swishing back and forth as they warily watched Flash.

"I don't want to be a referee and I don't want any violence," she told us. She certainly didn't look like a referee and I agreed with her views on violence.

Flash looked up and gave the other cats a threatening look and hissed at me. I edged backwards towards the steps. I thought my best course of action would be to get out of there pronto.

"Watch out!" warned Mr. Whiskers. "He doesn't know you and thinks you're a threat."

I was no threat to anyone, especially to this striped whirlwind. Flash puffed up his fur and flattened his ears as he continued to stare at me.

"You'd better make a run for it before he hurts you," Mr. Whiskers advised me.

The cat lady had stood up and had picked up a chair cushion to put between Flash and me in case he attacked.

"No, no!" she cried. "Leave the little cat alone!"

I slowly backed down the steps without turning my backside to Flash. He continued to make hostile-sounding noises and he was frightening me. I knew some cats will provoke other cats and then a rumble might break out and I didn't want to be the cause of that

"I'm leaving," I told Mr. Whiskers. "Sorry I couldn't get to know you any better."

"I'm sorry too, but Flash is so volatile, it's best for you to go now."

"Goodbye, my friend," I said. "Take care."

Flash started creeping in my direction and I took this as a sign to beat feet. I turned and ran down the street to find my destiny......again. I looked back and saw Flash crouched on the step sniffing where I had just been.

TIRED

Oh, I was tired. Tired of running away, tired of being chased, tired of trying to survive the cold, tired of living the wild life. I felt old. I was lonely. I had no friends, cat, dog, human or otherwise. I could have stayed close to the cat lady's house and made friends with the other cats but it was not to be. I had had my share of adventures and misadventures to last me the rest of my seven or eight lives that were left. All I wanted was to be able to lie down in the sun someplace where I was safe and loved. I wanted love. I wanted a soothing hand to stroke my fur and tickle me under the chin. I was even willing to let someone trim my claws. And brush my teeth...no, wait...maybe that was going too far. I wanted a predictable routine and a soft place to sleep. I was willing to give up my freedom and compromise by allowing someone make decisions for me.

But how was I going to accomplish this seemingly unreachable task? I was homeless, out on the street, just a cat with no prospects. I was a target for predators, mean people and merciless weather.

I crept under a bush in someone's yard and lay down. The ground was still cold but I turned my face to the rising sun. The morning sunlight cheered me up a bit and I decided to rest for a while. I must have dozed off but then awoke because I had a dream that was very vivid. In the dream, my friend Ivory was asking me to follow her as she made her way down a pathway that sparkled with dew. She was leading me up to a pleasant-looking cottage where the back door was standing open. I tried to stay with her but obstacles kept blocking my way. A fence was too tall to jump and a wall was too slippery to climb. I called out to her but she just kept moving toward the door. I called and called her name but she didn't look back. That's when I woke up. What did the dream mean? Did it mean anything? Had Ivory crossed the rainbow bridge and wanted me to do the same? No, certainly not. I wasn't ready for the bridge. I was in good health, and unless something unexpected happened, I hoped to live many more years. I shook my head and looked around and realized that I was still under the shrub. I was sad because I felt like I had just lost Ivory and my memory of her for good. I sighed a small cat sigh.

Two children came out of the house and walked down the street, presumably to catch a school bus. They didn't look my way. They were laden down with overflowing backpacks and I was glad I wasn't a child. But then, they had a nice home and probably people to care for them and feed them and protect them.

As the day warmed, I stretched and decided to explore the town a bit more. Turning down a side street, I followed the sidewalk as it curved around a bend. Taking notice of the houses, I perceived it to be a pleasant neighborhood with well-kept yards. A few early risers were out, puttering in their gardens, getting some exercise on their daily walk or leaving for work in their cars. I leisurely kept to the sidewalk, taking in the sweet smell of spring and the newness of the earth. Where was I going? I didn't know and I didn't really care. I didn't have a destination; I didn't have a purpose.

After a block or two, I came upon an agreeable-looking house, set back from the street. Something about this house looked familiar, but I knew I hadn't ever been here before. I stopped on the sidewalk and admired the well-tended grass and the blooming flowers. Something was drawing me nearer and nearer and I couldn't put my paw on it. I saw a little black face appear in one of the downstairs windows. The eyes were piercing and became round like an owl's eyes. The rest

of the body followed the black face around the curtain
and I could see it was a young cat, inspecting me closely.
The cat arched her back and bristled her bushy tail. I
figured the cat was a female; she just looked feminine.
She also looked like she had a big attitude even though
she was inside and I was outside. I sat down to watch
her. I thought to myself, aren't cats weird? Why do they
take an instant dislike to other cats when they don't
even know them? I hadn't done anything to this cat; I
was merely passing through the neighborhood. Black
One hissed silently at me and I laughed to myself. What
a clown, I thought.

Then a lady opened the curtains and picked up
Black One and cuddled her. Ah, another nice scene
where a cat is loved and looked after by a caring human. It reminded me of Scorpio and his human
housemate. Black One suddenly reached out and
grabbed the edge of the curtain, pulling at it so it
looked like it could possibly tear. The lady gently
took the cat's arm and disentangled the claws from
the curtain. At that moment, she turned her gaze
outside to where I was sitting and saw me sitting on
the sidewalk. I looked at her and saw her smile at
me. A minute or two later she opened the door and
came out onto the porch with a dish of cat food. She
placed the dish close to the stairs and then stepped
back to watch me. Since I hadn't had time to finish
my breakfast when Flash appeared at the other cat

lady's house, I went up to the porch and timidly began eating the food.

The lady spoke softly, "What's your name?"

I ignored her, not in a rude manner, but just kept munching.

"Did you just come for a visit and are only passing through?"

I continued to eat.

The lady sat down on the porch beside me and tentatively stroked my back. I didn't protest. Her touch was gentle and light.

"You could use a little attention, couldn't you?" she asked.

I thought, yes, I could use a LOT of attention.

The lady's dark hair shone in the sun and fell to her shoulders in an easy way. She wore jeans and a sweater and some tennis shoes. I could smell the fragrance of cats on her clothes and wondered whether she had any others living with her besides Black One. I didn't smell any dog scents. She stretched out her legs on the porch as she observed me.

I finished the food she had given me and began my morning ablutions. Even though I had lost weight and my fur wasn't as pretty as it once had been, I tried to keep myself in good condition. Since I really didn't have any place in particular to go, I took my time and felt comfortable in the lady's presence. She didn't seem like she was in a hurry to go anywhere either. She turned her face to the sun and closed her eyes as if she was recalling a pleasant memory. I did the same thing and tried to absorb some of the sun's healing rays. She didn't say anything and I didn't either. Presently she leaned back against the side of the porch and patted her lap and I moved over and put my front paws on it. I kneaded her leg without digging my claws into it and then I rested my head on the same leg and I could feel her relaxing and breathing slowly. We both took a short catnap together on her front porch.

Wow! I awoke refreshed even though it must have only been a few minutes I dozed. The lady hadn't moved but as I shifted my position she smiled at me again and petted my head.

"Whose cat are you? Where do you belong?"

I looked at her and wanted to tell her that I didn't belong to anyone or any place now. I was just a runaway, gone astray with no place to go. I rubbed against her arm and she pulled me close. A faint whiff of her sweater had a vaguely familiar smell but I couldn't imagine what it could be. Why did I feel so contented here? I didn't know this nice lady but she had a calm way about her that told me she knew cats and the ways of cats. What was the almost recognizable scent that lingered on her sweater? I inhaled and felt happy. I curled up on the porch and fell asleep. The lady went back inside her house.

I awoke later to the sound of cats quarreling. The noise was coming from inside the house and I looked up at the window and saw Black One staring at me. How many cats lived here? This definitely seemed to be a cat house and I wasn't sure whether I should stay on the porch or try to escape. At least they seemed to be indoor cats since I hadn't seen any outside. I didn't want to leave. I decided to play a little trick on Black One. I crept out of her range of sight and positioned myself directly underneath the window where she was sitting on the inside windowsill. All of a sudden I sprang up and briefly hung on the window screen, like the poster of a cat hanging from a tree limb that proclaimed, "Hang on baby, Friday's coming!" I was about five inches from Black One's face. I startled her so much that her eyes widened and her ears flattened. I laughed to myself and dropped back down to the porch. Luckily the window was closed. The next thing I knew, Black One had reared up on her hind legs and was scratching the windowpane. I figured she was actually playing with me. She wasn't so menacing after all. It was all bluff. I sat back and watched her trying to sharpen her claws on the window. I touched the screen with my paw and Black One touched the window on her side.

MARIANA

She heard the hissing from the kitchen where she was making herself a cup of tea. Following the low growling sounds, she saw Cassidy on the windowsill, peering outside with her tail fluffed.

She reached over and picked up her little black cat and asked her "What's wrong, Cass? Why the big tail so early in the morning?"

Cassidy just reached to grab the curtain and Mariana tried to extract the claws from the fabric.

"How about if you come on in the kitchen and I'll give you a squirt of whipped cream?"

Cassidy was still intent on whatever was outside. Her attention was riveted on the front yard. Mariana glanced out and that's when she saw the little calico, sitting in the yard, chin up with her tail wrapped around herself.

"Oh my. Now I see what you were so interested in," she told Cassidy. She carried Cassidy into the kitchen and just as she promised, took a small saucer and put a small dollop of whipped cream in it and set it on the floor. She then opened a small can of cat food and dished it out to take to the calico outside. She didn't think of the consequences or have any other thoughts except that the cat would probably be hungry.

Out on her porch, she talked soothingly to the furry stranger and put the food plate down. The cat seemed a bit shy and reluctant to eat so she sat down on the porch and gave the cat some room. She was thinking that it was such a pretty spring day, just the kind that her mother would have loved to celebrate her birthday. Today would have been her mother's birthday if she had still been living. Mariana closed her eyes and began remembering her sweet mother whom she had lost about fifteen years ago. She and her mom had always been close and enjoyed each other's company, sharing the same likes and dislikes. As far back as she could remember, her mother had taken in stray cats and turned them into pets. Mariana had learned much from her, watching the gentle and tender way her mom had treated each newcomer. How appropriate that today, of all days, a stray cat would show up in her yard.

When the calico was finished eating and washing, Mariana touched her and encouraged her to rest on her lap. It seemed such a natural thing to do and soon, they both semi-dozed off in the morning sun.

Cassidy had thrown a hissy fit when Mariana had gone outside to feed and pay attention to the calico.

"There's a CAT outside!" she shrieked. "A calico cat! Mariana's feeding it!" The other cats weren't impressed with this news. Sometimes neighborhood cats would come by to visit since they knew Mariana had a soft heart and loved all cats.

"Oh, so what?" Charlie said. "That's nothing new. Haven't you ever seen one before?"

"But she's sleeping on Mariana's lap!"

"Why don't you go sleep on Mariana's bed and let us take our morning naps, too?"

Mariana didn't have much planned for the day but she wanted to check on her cats so she went into the house to find them napping, Inbox in his favorite place, Lily curled up beside Charlie, Cassidy and Ivory on the bed.

She noticed the picture of her mother on the top of a bookcase and went over to it, staring at the familiar face.

"Oh, I wish you were still here. I miss you so!" she said to the photo. Her mother's name was Katherine, but everyone always called her Katie. The name Katie seemed so appropriate for the petite dark haired woman who might have been called a Cat Whisperer for her talent of taming stray and feral cats. Felines were drawn to her like a magnet. Mariana had inherited her love of cats from Katie.

Mariana looked out her front window and saw the calico was still resting on the porch. She thought that this cat was no feral and wondered if she belonged to one of her neighbors. She would wait and see whether the cat stayed or left tonight to go back home, wherever that may be. About mid-afternoon she opened the door and walked out on the porch only to find that the calico was gone. She looked around the yard but didn't see any sign of her.

"Well I hope she comes back," she said to herself. "We have room for one more if she wishes to stay."

I was hiding under a forsythia bush, which was ablaze in yellow petals, heralding the first days of spring. I watched the lady step out on her porch and look around. I was thinking that this might not be a bad place to land.

My thoughts reviewed the events of the past years as I imagined the next few years into the future. Memories came back to me of my first family who didn't care about me, my adventures in the shelter, and subsequent adoption by Monique. I thought about my escape into the woods and the close encounter with the coyote, of the man with the chainsaw, and finding Romeo's old homestead. For the hardships I had suffered in my travels, and almost starving during the winter, it was a miracle that I was still alive. Getting stuck in the fish truck had almost done me in.

On the pro side, I believed that I could find a good home here with the nice lady. I would have to abide by her rules and try to get along with the other cats who lived here. I wouldn't have to scrounge for food or evade predators or get run over on a city street. I wouldn't have to live in a cage and I thought that I would be well cared-for. The house looked like it had heat and I wouldn't freeze when winter came again. I had already used up several of my lives and I wasn't getting any younger so the remaining ones would probably be comfortable and peaceful.

On the con side, I would have to give up my freedom, the freedom to come and go wherever I wanted, when I wanted. I would become a complacent, and maybe even lazy middle-aged cat. I probably would gain weight from not exercising or running free. I might have to stay inside the house and not be able to climb trees or feel the wind in my fur. I would probably not have many exciting adventures anymore.

Was it worth it? Was my safety and well-being more important than allowing my cat instincts to guide me? Could I give up eating mice and birds? Oh, there were so many things to consider. I semi-napped under the forsythia while I listened to the chirps of early spring birds.

After a while, I got up, stretched, and went around to the back yard. I stopped in my tracks, stunned. There, in front of me, was a curving, paved pathway. It sparkled with dew but was quickly drying in the sun. There was a tall wall on one side, dividing the yard from the neighbor's. A fence on the other side of the yard separated it from an expanse of an open field. This scene was what I had dreamed of the night before! I could see the green beginnings of catnip coming up in the flower areas. The only thing that was missing was my friend, Ivory. She had been the one leading me down the path. It all looked so familiar and I remembered the dream vividly. And here it was, right before my eyes. I sat down to take all this in. Had I been projecting my thoughts into the future? Had I been wishing to see Ivory so much that I put her subconsciously in this situation? Was she here?? Did she live in this house??

I ran around to the front porch and stood on my hind legs and peered in the window where Black One had first spotted me.

"IVORY! IVORY! IVORY!" I called. "Are you here?"

There was another window at the end of the porch and I felt it pulling me toward it. As I went closer, I saw those beautiful green eyes, smiling at me. I saw Ivory, my long-lost best friend reach out her paw toward me. She was not on the other side of the rainbow bridge; she was right here in the house! I reached up to touch her on the outside of the window.

"Kitty! Is that you?" she asked through the window.

"Yes! I'm here!"

"I called you in my sleep and now, it's a miracle that you appeared."

I was shaken. Out of all the houses I could have chosen, I chose the one where Ivory lived. Was this a coincidence or fate? Did everything really happen for a purpose as I had heard? I was still not certain that this was real, that I was standing on the porch of the house where Ivory lived. All my doubts disappeared about whether to try to stay here or move on. There was nowhere else on earth I wanted to be or to live. My soul-mate was here and this is where I would be, until we had to cross the rainbow bridge.

A NEW NAME

I moved in that day. I never looked back. I never had any regrets. I realized that this was my destiny. Later that afternoon when Mariana opened the door again, I was waiting. I pushed by her and rushed into the foyer, looking around until I spotted Ivory across the room. I sprinted over to her and wrapped my arms around her. I kissed her face. I had never been so glad to see a cat as I was with Ivory. We nuzzled each other and stayed side by side as the other cats looked on, puzzled as to who this newcomer was, barging in on their territory. I sneaked a peek at Black One, who was eyeing me closely. Mariana just watched us silently.

This love scene went on for a while. I couldn't get enough of my pretty friend, who I noticed had put on a little weight but she looked great nevertheless.

I could hear the other cats murmuring.

"That's weird."

"It almost looks like Ivory knows this cat."

"Who is she?"

"Maybe they are related some way."

"They don't really look like each other."

"Get her out of here! We don't need any more cats here!" Cassidy shouted. "This is turning into a cathouse!"

"Where did she come from?"

Ivory finally spoke up and said, "This is Kitty, my old friend from the shelter. We've known each other for a long time and she has come to live with us. I love her and you will too when you get to know her."

"How do you know that Mariana will invite her to live with us?"

"Mariana is a cat person who can't resist any cats. And who could resist little Kitty?"

"I could!" Cassidy stated.

I finally said, "My name was changed from Kitty to Jazmine when I lived with my person and a dog."

"A dog!"

"Ha ha! You don't look like a Jazmine." Cassidy declared. "That name belongs to a cat who is classy and upscale."

Ivory told her, "Kitty or Jazmine as she is called now is classy and upscale. Just wait until she has lived with us and you'll see for yourself. Of course, Mariana doesn't know her name so she'll probably name her something else."

I said to Ivory, "I have so much to tell you about what has happened in my life. It will take days to tell you everything."

She replied, "Well, you'll have all the time you want. Why don't you go over and rub up against Mariana to let her know you like it here?"

"Yeah, good idea." So that's what I did and she then picked me up and looked deeply into my eyes.

"Sweetheart, I've never seen a cat act like you do toward Ivory. It's almost like you know each other. Maybe you did in one of your previous lives. You are welcome to stay here and become a part of our family if you wish."

I rubbed my face into her neck and nuzzled her. I purred in her ear and I could tell she loved that. I gently tapped her cheek with my claws sheathed and she smiled.

"What should we call you?" she asked. "Let me think about it for a while to see what I come up with."

I was thinking, "Just don't name me Kitty, please." But I would have been happy with any old name now that I was close to Ivory again. I still couldn't believe my good fortune in finding my friend. It must have been destiny that brought us together. How could I be so lucky?

I spent the rest of the afternoon close to Ivory. We talked and cuddled together. The other cats shook their heads in disbelief. She told them that she'd explain later. We curled up next to each other and reveled in being together. Every so often Mariana would come by and look at us. Once she sat on the floor and talked softly to me and to Ivory. I looked around the room and saw a few wooden plaques adorning some book-shelves with cat-related quotations on them. One was engraved with the words, *"Time spent with cats is never wasted."* ~Collette Another read, *"I love cats because I enjoy my home; and little by little, they become its visible soul."* ~Jean Cocteau

I had a feeling of utmost peace and belonging that I hadn't experienced since I lived with Monique and Buster. It was nice. I was happy and contented. The house smelled homey and pleasant. It was clean but not antiseptic.

I had always thought that I would never see Ivory again. She had thought the same thing about me. It just goes to show that one never knows what is going to happen in the future. You may think that something is inevitable, but then an incident happens to turn your world upside down. Good or bad, you have no control over what is in store for you. I will learn not to say never again.

I ignored Black One, whose name I learned was actually Cassidy after Ivory told me all the other cats' names. Cassidy had crouched down underneath a lo-veseat and watched us for a long time. I had a feeling she would be a problem to live with, but then I remem-bered our little game just hours before when we played through the window. I might be able to make friends with her eventually. The other cats went about their business throughout the day, not paying much attention to me, but not totally ignoring me either. Maybe I would fit in here with the residents.

I told Ivory about seeing Scorpio in the apartment window and she was happy that he found a good home. I also relayed the story of when I found Romeo's old homestead and my adventures with the shed dwellers.

She then told me about Spunky, the wild cat who had such a rough life and then calmed down somewhat while we were all in the shelter. Since Mariana volunteered sometimes at the shelter, she would work with all types of cats. Ivory said that one day she came home and she looked unhappy. She always would talk to her cats as if they knew what she was saying, which of course, they did. She related the story of one cat who had been returned to the shelter, after he had been taken home by one of the volunteers. She started to describe Spunky and Ivory perked up when she heard his name.

Mariana had said, "This cat they called 'Spunky' had been at the shelter before. He was the wildest of the wild and so incorrigible that everyone there was afraid of him. He was all beat up from banging around in the trap and no one could even go near him. Even the cats stayed away from him. The volunteers told me that a little cat had befriended him and that helped to calm him down, even to the point of one of the workers taking him home to try to tame him. Well, Spunky didn't adjust well to being in a house. He felt confined and he was continually meowing and acting up. Late one night he was awake as usual, prowling around the house and he decided to jump up on the fireplace mantel. There were a few items on the mantel, including a precious antique vase that had been given to the worker by a relative, long deceased. Spunky accidentally knocked it off the mantel, where it crashed to the tile floor, breaking into fifty million smithereens. The worker finally had enough of Spunky's shenanigans and took him back to the shelter."

Ivory and I just looked at each other. We were both thinking that Spunky had been progressing so well when we were there. What a shame that he was back in a cage, confined to a small space, which had nearly driven him crazy before.

Mariana continued, "They want me to work with him to see if he can be tamed. I seem to be the only one who has enough patience to help him overcome his anxiety. I hope he will come around so someday he might be adopted by the right person."

Ivory could tell she was depressed at the thought of Spunky being returned to the shelter.

Ivory said to me, "Maybe when we know Mariana is going to the shelter, you can mark her and make sure your scent is on her clothes. It's a possibility that

Spunky will smell you and remember how you made life easier for him for a while."

I told her, "Yes, I'll definitely do that. Poor Spunky. Someday he'll find someone who understands cats and will take him home. We have to think positively about that."

At dinner that night, I could tell that Mariana was considering me. She would walk around me like she was sizing me up. I was eating out of my own dish, close to the other cats. They seemed to be accepting me, except for Cassidy who hissed periodically. What a silly cat she was!

When it was time for Mariana to go to bed, she took me aside and began stroking my back. She took my face in both hands and kissed me on my forehead.

"You are like a gift from heaven. I don't know how you found us, but it's like you have belonged here for a long time. It's almost unbelievable how happy you've made Ivory today. You must have been friends in a former life. Oh, how I wish that you could talk and tell me everything. There must be some great stories in your past."

I thought, "Yes, indeed. I also wish that I could talk in your language, but since I can't, I will try to communicate in other ways that will convey what I want to tell you."

She then uttered the words I had been waiting for. "I've been thinking about an appropriate name for you.

Since you appeared on my mother's birthday, I think I'll name you Katie, after her. She would be honored to have her namesake move in with us."

Katie! Katie! I loved it! Not Jazmine, not Kitty. I was now Katie! I reached up and kissed Mariana softly on her cheek.

THE END

EPILOGUE

So what happened to some of the cataracters in Gone Astray?

Kitty's first family was happy with their new puppy and eventually added another dog to their family, which the boys loved. They were able to romp and play with the dogs unlike they could with Kitty when she lived with them.

The chainsaw man saw the need to revise his eating habits and exercise more without exerting himself to an extreme. He developed a sense of kindheartedness toward cats and he and his wife eventually adopted one from the shelter. He always remembered the little calico who had revived him after his unfortunate episode in the woods.

The old farmer moved into a retirement village where he could putter around in his small yard. He planted a few tomatoes in the sunny back yard and one day when a stray black cat made himself at home in his garden, the farmer decided to befriend him and then shared his life and home with the furry one.

Romeo lived with his adoptive family and was truly happy. The stylish lady had two children at home and the friendly cat made a good addition to the family.

Romeo avoided the bathtub and the sinks in the bathrooms as he had no fascination with water.

Scorpio adored his human companion. Apartment living agreed with him and his human pampered him like he was used to when he previously lived like a king.

Spunky was returned to the shelter and was viewed as an incorrigible. He was maladjusted and sulked in his cage. Volunteers tried to turn him into an adoptable cat, but most were unable to make any headway. However, Spunky did finally get a break and his life began to change, following an unexpected event.

Buster continued to run and play in heaven. He was reunited with his former cat housemates and his dog friends from the park. His body was young and supple again and he had ample opportunity to frolic in the surf at the heavenly beach.

Monique adjusted to life in the Air Force. She became an airman and was sent to Germany to live and pursue her career for a few years. She continued to remember her sweet cat, Jazmine and hoped that she had been fortunate in her life.

Mariana let her life revolve around her cat family. She loved all her cats and made sure each one was given equal attention. She marveled at the bond between Ivory and Katie. A valuable volunteer at the shelter, she worked with cats that had a bad start in their lives.

Ivory was ecstatic that her long-gone friend had showed up at her house and moved in. She purred constantly and shared the love with her other cat companions. Much time was spent grooming Katie and sleeping close to her. They shared a special bond that no one ever quite understood.

Katie was the perfect picture of contentment. Her beautiful orange, black and white coat was glossy and soft. Her eyes reflected her happiness. She would jump up on a windowsill to watch the birds and other wildlife outdoors and she never had a thought of trying to return to her former life as a stray. Once a stray and now home to stay!

Made in the USA
Columbia, SC
11 August 2019